Also by Helena S. Paige

Coming soon:

A Girl Walks into a Wedding

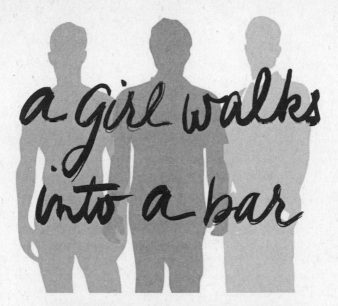

a girl walks into a bar

YOUR FANTASY, YOUR RULES

Helena S. Paige

WM

WILLIAM MORROW
An Imprint of HarperCollinsPublishers

A GIRL WALKS INTO A BAR. Copyright © 2014 by Helena S. Paige. All rights
reserved. Printed in the United States of America. No part of this book may
be used or reproduced in any manner whatsoever without written permis-
sion except in the case of brief quotations embodied in critical articles and
reviews. For information address HarperCollins Publishers, 10 East 53rd
Street, New York, NY 10022.

HarperCollins books may be purchased for educational, business, or sales
promotional use. For information please e-mail the Special Markets Depart-
ment at SPsales@harpercollins.com.

FIRST EDITION

Designed by Diahann Sturge

Library of Congress Cataloging-in-Publication Data has been applied for.

ISBN 978-0-06-229197-4

14 15 16 17 18   OV/RRD   10 9 8 7 6 5 4 3 2 1

How to Get the Most Fun Out of This Book

Dear Reader,

This isn't a regular novel with a set beginning, middle, and end. This is your story, and you're in charge. Of your life, your sexuality, your fantasies.

So here's how it works: At the end of every scene, you'll be given a choice, with instructions to go to the page that corresponds with your selection. It's simple: YOU pick what you want to do, where you want to go, who you want to be with. There are no right or wrong decisions. Just keep going through to the pages, and you're guaranteed a wild ride that you shape and control.

Wondering "what if"? Want to try something different? Unlike in life, here you can press a reset button. Just go back to the previous fork in the road, pick something different, and head out on a new adventure.

Because remember: it's your fantasy, your rules.

Enjoy!

Helena S. Paige

a girl walks
into a bar

ALL WOMEN KNOW THAT you can't expect too much from a single pair of underwear. If you want drop-dead sexy, you're going to have to sacrifice on the comfort front. If it's pure comfort you're after, it's unlikely you'll be wearing anything particularly pretty or glamorous. If you're in need of support, then control-top is your friend, but you aren't going to be breathing very easily.

You let your towel slip to the floor and lean naked over your underwear drawer to consider your options. You and your best friend, Melissa, have been threatening to paint the town red for weeks—chances are it's going to be a big night. There's the ridiculously expensive purple lace G-string with the silk ribbon woven along the edges. You run your fingers over one of the velvety ribbons and feel a little nostalgic—you haven't worn sexy undies in ages.

Next to them are your favorite most-comfy pant-ies. The elastic isn't as tight as it used to be, and they're slightly faded from all that washing, but that's kind of what you like about them.

Instinctively you suck in your stomach as you reach for the control-top underwear. They make you feel like you're crammed into a sausage skin, but at least they give you a flat stomach. But what if you get lucky tonight? You'll need a can opener to get out of them, and there's nothing sexy about that. Maybe you should just go commando, you think. You smile a little at the thought. You've never done that before. Wouldn't it be incredibly sexy to be the only one who knows you're not wearing anything under your dress?

- If you choose the purple lacy G-string, go to page 3.

- If you choose the comfy panties, go to page 4.

- If you choose the control-top underwear, go to page 5.

- If you choose to go commando, go to page 7.

Helena L. Paige

✎ You've chosen the purple lacy G-string

🍸 YOU DO SOME FINAL touch-ups to your makeup in the mirror, then step back to appraise the view. Work has been so hectic, it's been ages since you glammed up like this, and you'd forgotten what fun it can be. The little black dress with the low-cut neckline showcases your curves, and these are your favorite heels—they give you the calves and height of a goddess. You're pleased with what you see: the purple G-string was absolutely the right choice. Who knows, tonight might just be the night you break your drought. You might just get lucky.

✎ Go to page 8.

✎ You've chosen the comfy panties

🍹 You CHECK YOURSELF OUT in the mirror. It's a good look, the little black number with black high heels. You're feeling pretty sexy tonight for the first time in ages. You turn around to check the back of your dress and catch a glimpse of your granny–panty line marring the smooth fabric of your dress. Nope, that won't do. You whip off the granny panties and briefly consider going commando . . .

✎ If you want to go commando, go to page 7.

. . . but you decide against it. That's a little too breezy for your liking. Instead, you open the drawer again and reach for the purple lacy G-string. You climb into it, careful not to snag it on a high heel.

✎ Go to page 3.

🖎 *You've chosen the control-top underwear*

YOU HAVE TO LIE on the bed to get into your control-top underwear. Who invented them? Clearly a sadist who doesn't like women very much. And what are they made out of–the same fabric they use in space shuttles? You take a deep breath, hold it, and drag the underwear past your thighs.

Just before you pass out from lack of oxygen, you manage to heave them over your tummy. Wiping a bead of sweat off your face, you scramble up and check yourself in the mirror. On the upside, your stomach is flat. Unnaturally so—it's almost concave. On the downside, you feel a little dizzy, you might have cracked a rib, and you probably won't be able to sit down all night.

Who said beauty is supposed to hurt? Something's got to give. You grab a pair of scissors and cut yourself out of the Lycra straitjacket, breathing out with relief.

Then you reach for the purple G-string instead and

slip it up your legs. After the industrial-strength Lycra, the lace feels like feathers. You hold your breath as you look in the mirror, and it has the same effect as the sadistic underwear, but without cutting off your circulation. You'll just have to remember to suck in your stomach every time someone looks at you, you think as you reach for your handbag.

∽ Go to page 8.

Helena L. Paige

❧ You've chosen to go commando

You walk to the kitchen to pour yourself some wine, swinging your hips. It feels strange not to be wearing anything under your dress. The friction of your thighs pressing against each other as you walk feels good. In fact, every move you make is a bit of a turn-on. You've never been this aware of your nethers. So this is what it must be like for guys, you think—your sexuality reminding you that it's there with every move you make.

You take your glass back to the bedroom. Just that short walk has made heat flood through your body. It's too much, you think. You won't make it to the bar at this rate. You decide you need something between you and your dress if you're going to be able to look anyone in the eye tonight without blushing violently. You reach for the minimal purple G-string—it's the next best thing to going naked.

❧ Go to page 3.

‰ Arriving at the bar

‰ You have to blink a few times as your eyes adjust to the dim lighting inside the bar. The background music is subtle, but you can feel the rhythmic beat in your chest, along with a pleasant quiver of expectation. You've been so focused on work, it's been a while since you went out. You have every intention of having fun tonight.

You've never been here before; this trendy celebrity hangout was Melissa's idea, and you gaze around, hoping to spot her. A long mahogany bar counter stretches along the length of one side of the room, and groups of stylishly dressed people are laughing and lounging at the booths and tables. There's a roped-off area at the back, with a bouncer the size of Conan the Barbarian parked in front of it. It must be the VIP section. No chance you'll ever get in there, you think.

You scope out the bar, but there's no sign of Melissa, so

you check the tables. You can't help noticing a striking man sitting at one of the booths in the corner. He's deep in conversation with another guy, but something about him tugs at you. He's clearly a little older than you, but he makes it look good in a George Clooney kind of way. He looks up and catches your eye, as if sensing your attention. His stare is intense. You blush and make a show of looking at your watch, as much to check the time as to have an excuse to look away from him. It's five past eight. You're on time. Where the hell is Melissa?

You take one more careful look around the room, then make your way over to the bar and perch on a stool, your back to Mr. Intense. You shiver—you can almost feel the pressure of his gaze on your back.

"Hi, what can I get you?" asks the bartender.

You glance up, taken aback at how attractive he is, even if he looks barely old enough to be serving alcohol. His skin is flawless, set off by espresso-colored hair and eyes. He's wearing jeans and a plain white cotton shirt, and he smiles sweetly, if a little hesitantly, as he snags an empty can off the bar counter next to you. Then in one smooth move he turns and tosses it into the trash, getting it in the first time. His crisp white cotton sleeves are rolled up, revealing the sculpted muscles in his arms. You can't help wondering how old he is—twenty-one, twenty-two at a guess. Hmm. You could show him a thing or two.

You're not sure what to order. This is a celeb hangout, after all. Champagne? A cocktail? A martini? Then you remember a scene you saw in a movie. "A glass of

a girl walks into a bar

prosecco, please," you say, hoping you pronounced it correctly.

The bartender flicks his hair out of his eyes and gives you that sweet and rather shy smile again. It floors you for the second time.

"Coming right up." He reaches for a champagne glass. His shirt lifts and you get a perfect view of his smooth, muscled stomach. A dark line of silky hair runs from just below his navel to the button of his jeans. You can't help it—your mouth waters a little. Where's Melissa? She needs to see this. Good choice of bar, you'll tell her. You cross your legs and squeeze them together.

Your cell phone vibrates in your hand, startling you. It's a text from Melissa:

> Stuck at work, Evil Boss sprang horror deadline on me. Sorry! So upset I can't make it. ☹ Have fun for me! ☺

Your heart sinks. Now what? You thump your phone down. All dressed up with nowhere to go. If only she'd let you know earlier. When will Melissa learn to say no to her controlling bastard of a boss?

You're not even sure you're in the mood for a drink anymore, but the cute bartender is already expertly opening a bottle of sparkling wine. He pours a glass, holding it at a slant, then puts it down in front of you with another shy smile, and you cheer up a little. You wonder what it would feel like to run a thumb along the

Helena S. Paige

10

line of his lips, which are full and temptingly kissable. You smile back at him and reach for your bag to pay.

"No, no need," he says.

Is he coming on to you? You're about to thank him when he points to the far end of the bar, an apologetic look on his face. "It's from that guy over there."

You check out your admirer. His garish shirt is open to his midriff, and there's more hair on his chest than on his head. A thick gold chain nestles in the thicket above the beginnings of a hefty paunch. He pops a toothpick in his mouth, gets up, and swaggers his way over to you. Maybe if you don't make eye contact, this walking cliché will get the message . . . No such luck.

"Hello, darlin'," he says, shifting the toothpick from side to side with his tongue. "This seat taken?" He plonks himself down next to you before you have a chance to answer. "I'm Stanley Glenn," he says, as if he expects you to recognize the name. A burp slips out of his mouth, and garlic wafts toward you. You lean as far back as you can, but there's no escaping it. "Pardon me, but better out than in, right? That's what I always say." He holds up both hands, points his fingers, and fires them off at you with a wink and a double-click of the mouth.

Your first instinct is to tell him and his chest wig to get lost, but that would be rude, and you don't want to make a scene. But you shift in your seat so you can knee him in the nuts if he comes any closer with that lethal breath of his. You're about to politely decline the drink when you feel a hand on your shoulder. Startled, you

swivel to face a man standing just behind you. You recognize him immediately: it's the guy who caught your eye when you first arrived at the bar.

"Hello, sweetheart, sorry I'm late," he says, leaning forward and kissing you on the cheek. You suck in a breath at the unexpected closeness. He smells like cedar and leather, and this close, you can see the sexy salt-and-pepper at his temples and the smile lines at the corners of his eyes.

Keeping one arm draped casually over your shoulder, he holds out his other hand to Stanley. "Thank you so much for keeping her company. Running a little late. Business stuff, you know how it goes."

Aware that you're shamelessly taking advantage of the situation, you lean back a little against your rescuer's arm. Chest Wig mumbles something and gets to his feet. As they shake hands, you notice that Stanley winces. The toothpick disappears, and you wonder if he's swallowed it. His face puce, Chest Wig backpedals out of sight.

"Hi, I'm Miles," says your new acquaintance, lifting his arm from your shoulder.

"And I'm grateful," you say, your skin still tingling where he touched you.

"I hope that wasn't too presumptuous of me?"

"I could have handled it, but thanks for the help," you smile.

"I have no doubt you could have dispatched him with a single look if you'd wanted to," he says. "But I needed an excuse to come over and introduce myself."

Helena S. Paige

This sounds promising, and you're about to offer to buy him a drink when he goes on: "It was very nice to meet you, but I'd better get back to my colleague; we're just finishing up a bit of business."

"Oh, right." You don't want him to leave, but you don't know how to ask him to stay. "Thanks again."

"It's my pleasure." He gazes at you for another long second before turning to go back to his table. You watch him walk away. He's wearing exquisitely cut trousers and a shirt with the faintest blue pinstripe, open at the collar. Stylish and clearly not cheap. He turns, catches you checking him out, and raises his hand in a wave. You smile back and then turn to your bubbly for a big sip, your mouth dry.

"Another one?" asks the young bartender as you drain your glass. The bubbles are delicious, but you're thirsty, so you ask for Perrier.

"Prosecco, Perrier—you're in a Mediterranean mood," says the bartender, surprising you. That's not normal bar chat, and you look at him more closely. Even in the dim, artificial lighting, his skin glows.

"So what's a nice guy like you doing in a place like this?" you say, feeling a little flirty—blame it on the bubbly.

"Splitting a shift with my cousin; he's the regular bartender here. The money helps—textbooks are expensive."

"Oh, you're a student?"

"Yes, and please don't ask me what I'm studying . . ."

"Well, I wasn't going to, but now you've got me curious."

a girl walks into a bar

He looks a little sheepish. "Philosophy of religion. Especially Eastern religions."

"Really? I can't imagine that opens up a whole bunch of career options."

He looks serious for a moment. "You'd be surprised. I'd like to work in international peacekeeping at some point, maybe end up at the UN. Travel the world, you know."

Interestinger and interestinger. The face of an angel, the body of a sinner, and a brain as well? Plus he really does want world peace.

You give him a slow, promising smile. It may be cradle robbing, but you're tempted to pursue this a bit more. But first you'd better head to the ladies' room. If you're going to flirt with a seriously cute twenty-something, you should probably check your makeup.

The ladies' room is an oasis of calm and soft lighting. There's only one other woman in here with you, and she's busy at the mirror, applying makeup.

She is easily one of the most dramatic-looking women you've ever seen. Her glossy hair is piled up in loose ringlets on her head and pinned with a coral comb. Her brows almost meet in the middle, and she has a beauty spot low down on one cheek. Her long skirt is draped on her hips, the jewel-colored fabric catching the light. Vintage for sure, maybe even Valentino. She looks up from what she's doing and appraises you in the mirror, then smiles, as if she likes what she sees. You can't help but notice her breasts in her clinging lace top:

either she's impervious to gravity or she is wearing the most expensively engineered bra known to womankind.

In the beam of her calm gaze, you feel a bit drab in your little black number, like a pigeon who has strayed into the peacock enclosure.

"I'm sorry, I'm hogging the mirror," she says. Her voice has a little growl in it, or is that a hint of an accent?

"No, no, it's fine. I'm just going to use the facilities," you say, feeling awkward next to her elegance and self-possession. She smiles at you again, and you escape into a stall, your heart racing. You can't get that beauty spot out of your mind.

When you're done, you wash your hands and join her at the mirror to fix your makeup. Your eyeliner has smudged, and you could do with some lipstick.

"I love your hair," she says as you fish a comb out of your bag.

"Thank you," you say, bringing a hand up to your head self-consciously. "Funnily enough, I'd kill to have hair like yours."

"Isn't that always the way?" she says. "We all want what we can't have." She holds your eyes for a moment too long, and you're shocked to find yourself momentarily imagining running your tongue over that beauty spot. Where did that come from?

"Wait, you've got a little . . . Here, let me," she says, and, turning to you, she holds your chin with a firm hand and uses a tissue to wipe away the smudged liner under your eyes. Her face is so close to yours you can

a girl walks into a bar

15

barely breathe, but you're hyperaware of her scent, an exotic blend of spices.

Then she reaches into her makeup bag for an eye-liner pencil and one of those eye-shadow palettes. She holds them up in front of you. "You don't mind, do you? Close your eyes for me."

Unsure exactly what she's asking, you do as she says. You shiver a little as she strokes the eyeliner along the edge of your lids, then uses the pad of her finger to work it in a little. Then she repeats the process, this time with the slate-colored eye shadow and contrasting highlighter, delicately blending the fine powder onto your eyelids and up onto the brow bone. Her touch on your skin is incredibly soft, and you're beginning to feel a little light-headed.

You're hit with a sting of regret as she pulls away. "There," she says. "You're really something, *chica*," and she points at the mirror. You turn to look. Thanks to your new smoky lids, your eyes look far larger than they have any right to be. It's a vast improvement on your own amateur efforts. You wonder if your mysterious friend is a model of some kind.

"You look like you might appreciate this. Here." She extends a slim arm, weighted with silver bracelets, and wraps your fingers around a folded-up piece of paper. "It's been good meeting you. I hope you'll come," she says as she picks up her bag and walks toward the bathroom door, her hips swinging confidently.

"Thank you for doing my eyes," you say, a moment too late.

Once she's gone, you unfold the paper she pressed into your hand. It's an advertisement for an exhibition at an art gallery close by. The image is a closely cropped portrait of a woman's face, and you realize that it's actually her staring out, challenging you with those fabulous eyes. You run your finger over the word "Immaculata" at the bottom of the page. Is that her name? The name of the show? Is she the artist?

You slide the flyer into your handbag and step back out into the bar, but there's no sign of her—she must have left.

You go back to your stool, a little forlorn. You feel exposed, all dressed up with no one to talk to. The gorgeous bartender is dealing with a noisy group down at the end of the bar, and the intense man you encountered earlier is still nose-to-nose with his colleague. You could stick around and have one last drink, or there's always the option of the exhibition . . . there are sure to be canapés, at least.

❧ If you decide to stay, have another drink, and see what happens, go to page 18.

❧ If you decide to check out the exhibition at the gallery, go to page 52.

a girl walks into a bar

❧ You've decided to stay in the bar, have another drink, and see what happens

THE ANGEL-FACED BARTENDER IS heading back your way with the Perrier you forgot you'd ordered. You thank him and type a text to Melissa telling her she owes you one for standing you up.

"Excuse me," says a very deep voice. You look up from your phone at a massive tree of a man. He must be almost seven feet tall, and at least half that wide. He's dressed in a black suit, and a small wire is attached to an earpiece buried in his ear.

"I'm not sure if you noticed, but the Space Cowboys are here." He points a thumb over his shoulder, indicating the VIP area.

"They are?" you say, twirling around on your stool and craning your neck to see. The entourage must have arrived while you were in the ladies' room, and now the VIP area is heaving. Two waitresses are heading that way

18

with buckets of champagne, and another gorilla of a bouncer is standing guard outside the red ropes, making sure only the most important or beautiful people get in. You catch a glimpse of Jerry, the lead singer, who's got two tall model types draped over his shoulders. He wears blondes like you would wear a jacket.

"Yup," the bodyguard says. "Charlie asked me to come over and invite you up to the VIP area for a drink with him."

"He did?" You're astonished. It must be the eyes the woman in the bathroom gave you. If you ever see her again, you must remember to thank her. "He's the drummer, right?" you ask, peering at the VIP section to see if you can spot him. Yes, there he is, sitting on a leather couch next to the guitarist, whose name you can't remember. He catches your eye, smiles, and raises a hand.

You sit up straight and reach for your Perrier, wishing you had something stronger.

"I'm very flattered," you say. "But you can tell Charlie from the Space Cowboys that if he wants me to join him, he can get off his butt and come down here into the real world with the peasants, and ask me himself. Not send his bodyguard to do his dirty work for him. No offense!" you quickly add to the elephant in the room.

"None taken," says the huge man, and you think you detect a small smile at the corners of his mouth. "You *do* know who he is, right?"

"I don't care if he's Prince effing William," you say. "Tell him if he wants me, he knows where to find me."

Then you lean past the giant, make eye contact with Charlie across the room again, smile your most evil sexy smile, and raise your glass in a toast.

"All right," says Man-Mountain, this time with a definite smile.

You turn back to face the bar, your hands trembling slightly.

The VIP area is reflected in the mirror behind the bar, and if you turn your head a little, you can watch what's happening. You see the bouncer return to the VIP area and lean down to whisper something in Charlie's ear. At first he raises his eyebrows, then he looks taken aback, then he looks over at you. You act nonchalant, but you make sure you're sitting up with your tummy sucked in. Charlie leans back and starts to laugh. Seconds later he's up off the leather couch and your stomach does a backflip as you watch his reflection walk out of the VIP area and toward the bar. He's coming over to you—better practice your surprised face.

Most people go for the lead singer of a group, but there's something about the drummer that always gets you. Maybe it's because they tend to be such bad boys. Charlie has longish hair that falls in a jagged fringe over one eye. He's tall and lean, his arms laced with tattoos. One has a single sentence scrawled down the length of it. The hairs on the back of your neck do the Wave as you imagine trailing a finger over the letters.

"Hi," he says, leaning back against the bar next to you. He puts his hand out. "Nice to meet you. I'm Prince fucking William."

You had planned on playing it cool, but you can't help yourself—you burst out laughing. You shake his hand, aware of your damp palm. Your fingers are swallowed by his. "Your hands are enormous!" you blurt out, then mentally kick yourself for thinking out loud.

"Ah," he says, holding out his hands and examining them thoughtfully. "You know what they say about men with big hands, don't you?"

You blush furiously.

"Hey now, what were you thinking, you dirty girl? I meant they make great drummers!"

"Oh, is that what they say?" With a sudden rush of courage, you reach for one of his hands, cradling it in your palms. "Seriously, you truly do have the biggest hands I've ever seen. Have you been in touch with *Guinness World Records*? And if this is your Lifeline, you're going to be around for a really, really long time," you say, turning one hand over and tracing the line gently with a finger.

"You should see my feet," he says. Then he turns and surveys the bar. "So, is this what it's like down among the peasants?"

"Welcome to the real world. It's not often someone approaches me on behalf of someone else. It sort of took me back to junior high."

"You're right, it was a bit arrogant of me. How about you let me buy you a drink to make it up to you? Although I might need my hand back, just to pay, you know."

You realize you're still clutching his hand, and drop

a girl walks into a bar

it like a hot coal. Your head feels light and fizzy, just like the champagne. "That would be great, thank you."

Charlie beats out a quick rhythm on the bar counter. The young bartender approaches and tries not to do a double take when he realizes who it is: "What can I get you?"

Charlie looks down at you, his eyes flashing with mischief. "Two shots of gold tequila. With orange, not lemon."

You're about to protest that you're drinking sparkling wine, not tequila, but he cocks an eyebrow at you, and you suddenly realize you're about to drink tequila with the drummer from the Space Cowboys. He's easily one of the hottest guys in the bar, maybe even in the country, and he has those hands, those enormous, sexy hands, and he wants to drink tequila with you. This is one of those through-the-looking-glass moments that happens once in a lifetime. When you either seize the moment and do something a little crazy, or you don't, and possibly live to regret it.

Should you do it? You know exactly what tequila does to you, especially on top of sparkling wine—all your inhibitions fly out the window. If you go down this road, there's probably no turning back.

At the thought of partying with him, something deep inside you clenches. You smile back at Charlie and nod ever so slightly, trying to seem composed while inside you're sparking like a string of cheap Chinese fireworks. You wonder what happened to your Mr. In-

Helena S. Paige

22

tense, the suave older guy. He couldn't be more of a contrast to Charlie.

While you're still wavering, the bartender pours out the shots and balances half a slice of orange on top of each glass. Charlie slides yours over to you and holds his up in a challenging toast.

❧ If you want to drink tequila with a rock star,
go to page 24.

❧ If you don't want to drink tequila with a rock star,
go to page 44.

a girl walks into a bar

 WHY NOT? IT's NOT like you're going to settle down with this guy. There's no riding off into the sunset or white picket fence here—you see it for exactly what it is. If you play your cards right, this might be a happily-ever-after just for the night.

"Here's to Prince fucking William," says Charlie, clinking his shot glass against yours. You do the shot, screwing up your face as the liquor fires through your mouth and down your throat, then you suck on the orange to offset the burn of the tequila. Charlie laughs at the face you pull as he slams his own empty glass down on the bar and sucks on his orange.

"Ever do a body shot?" he asks.

You shake your head, feeling a rush of heat as the tequila makes its way through your system.

He moves a little closer. He somehow manages to

exude sex from every pore—he even smells like sex, you think—sex and tequila. He stretches out an arm and tucks a strand of hair behind your ear. You tingle at his touch, and you can barely take your eyes off his arm—you can almost feel the heat radiating from it.

"The rules to doing a body shot are simple," he says, leaning toward you, and there's that knowing grin again. You're so close you could almost kiss him. "I hold the orange in my mouth and you can put the salt wherever you want on my body, right? Then you lick the salt off me, down the shot, and bite the orange out of my mouth. Wanna do one?"

You don't trust yourself to speak, so you simply nod. Your panties are instantly wet at the thought of licking his body.

"Another four tequilas, please," Charlie says to the barman, "and this time we're going to need some salt."

Four? What have you gotten yourself into?

The barman pours out the shots and sets them in front of you. Charlie reaches for the saltshaker and hands it to you.

"You go first," he says, a challenge in his eyes. "What part of my body do you want?"

You take your time looking him up and down, but this decision is an easy one: it has to be that taut, muscled drummer's arm.

"Give me your arm," you say. You're impressed at how confident your voice sounds. You can feel your nipples hard and tight, brushing against the lace of your bra.

Charlie smiles his approval and reaches for a wedge

of orange, clamping the skin between his perfect teeth, the flesh of the fruit protruding, waiting for you. Then he holds his left arm out to you, the one without the writing on it.

You reach for it; his skin feels hot under your fingertips. Holding his gaze, you pour a stripe of salt down his forearm. You drop your head and, without breaking eye contact, you lick the salt from his arm in a line, making your tongue as wide and flat as you can so you can taste as much of his skin as possible. Then you go back for a second lick, to make sure you didn't miss a single grain of salt. He smells of musk and tastes like sweat.

His eyes are wide and his pupils dilate as he watches your tongue run over his arm. Then you reach for the shot and down it, and he leans toward you so that you can bite into the orange clamped between his lips. You clutch the back of his neck with your hand, pulling him close. You can feel his mouth pressing against yours as you bite into the orange.

You sit back, and he drops his huge hand onto your leg and squeezes it gently. The tequila, his closeness, his hand on your thigh, and the taste of him make your whole body quiver. Your mouth is puckering at the tartness of the orange, chasing the power of the tequila.

"My turn," Charlie says, staring into your eyes and licking his lips. You're so wet, if he had to touch you right now, right there, you'd probably come in seconds.

"I think I want your neck," he says slowly, still not taking his eyes off you. You gulp as he reaches out and

Helena L. Paige

pushes your hair away from your shoulder, brushing your neck with his fingers. "Right here," he says. Goose bumps explode all over your body. He leans even closer.

"I'd better lick it first," he says, "just to make sure the salt sticks, you know?"

You nod, your skin aching for more of those strong, clever fingers. You lean your head sideways so he has as much access to your neck as possible. With one hand steadying the other side of your neck, he runs his tongue from the dip of your collarbone all the way up the side of your neck, ending just below your ear. Then he pulls back and places the orange between your teeth, ready for his mouth. He pours the salt in a line across the licked skin. Then he holds your arms gently at your sides and licks up the strip of salt, starting at the dip of your neck and shoulder once again and running his hot tongue upward, lapping the salt off your skin. If he doesn't stop soon, it's completely possible you're going to come just from the feel of his tongue on your neck.

"I think I missed a spot," he mumbles into your ear. He goes back down to the edge of your collarbone again, and then he takes small nibbling bites all the way back up your neck. You think you might pass out from the sheer pleasure of it. Satisfied that he's licked you thoroughly, he shoots the tequila, then pulls you toward him again as he bites into the orange you're holding in your mouth. He holds his mouth against yours, and you can taste the salt and the tequila on his lips.

Far too soon, he pulls away from you. "What do you

a girl walks into a bar

say we go back to my hotel and find a few more interesting parts of our bodies to shoot tequila off of?" he says,
slamming his empty shot glass down on the counter.

❧ If you go back to the rock star's hotel to do
   more body shots, go to page 29.

❧ If you decide to walk away from the rock star,
   go to page 44.

❧ You've chosen to go back to the rock star's
hotel suite

❦ You're kneeling on the floor on a shag rug in front of a massive rock-star-type fireplace. It's a cliché, but it's a delicious cliché. Only a rock star would stay in a suite like this one. It covers one entire floor of the hotel, and boasts every imaginable luxury. There is music pumping at just the right level from invisible speakers that must be housed in the ceiling as well as the walls. The track is something you don't recognize, with a deep, smooth bass.

Charlie is kneeling in front of you. He lifts your dress up over your head in one smooth movement before you're even fully aware of what he's done. Then he gently pushes you back onto the shag rug, which feels soft and plush on your naked back.

"Lie still," he orders, "this won't hurt a bit." His voice is husky, and you shiver as he drips tequila into your belly button. "Now, where oh where shall I put the salt?" he teases, trailing his fingers down from your belly button to the edge of the purple lacy G-string.

"First rule of body shots," he says, snapping his fingers back just as you're starting to enjoy them, "no hands!" Then he bends his head down and pulls the edge of your bra down gently with his teeth—it grazes past your nipple as he pulls the lace away. You suck in a breath at the roughness of his teeth, your nipple so hard and sensitive you want to wriggle, but you can't because of the tequila pooled in your navel. Once he's tugged your bra away from your right breast, he sticks out his tongue and glides it in a generous lap across your taut nipple. Then he reaches for a wedge of sliced orange, holding it out for you to take in your mouth.

He blows gently on your breast where he's just licked, making your nipple even harder, the cool breath giving you goose bumps all over your burning body; then he pours a line of salt across the nipple, which is aching for his attention again.

Finally, just as you can barely stand to not be touched for another second, he leans in and licks the salt off your breast quickly—too quickly for your liking; you'd prefer him to stay there for a while longer—then drops his head down to your belly button. You can't help arching your back as he sucks the tequila out of your navel, his tongue dipping into it, twirling around the edges. Then, before your body knows what's hit it, he's straddling the length of you on all fours, his arms on the floor on either side of your head, and he drops his mouth onto yours,

Helena L. Paige

hungrily devouring the orange, and you don't know what happens to it or the rind, but it's gone in seconds, and then he's kissing you, and you can feel his cock hard through his jeans and against your panties, which are entirely soaked through.

You kiss frantically, furiously, your tongues entwining, full of the taste of salt and tequila. You push your hips up against his crotch, desperate for the relief of some friction. And then you wrap your naked legs around him, pushing against the hardness in his jeans. Enough of all these clothes—you really want to feel his skin against yours, so you roll him over onto his back and straddle him. Quick as a fox he reaches behind you and unsnaps your bra, freeing your breasts. But this isn't fair: you're almost entirely naked and he's still wearing almost all his clothes. So you grab his wrists and push his arms up behind his head. He tries to nip at your breasts, but you want to tease him a bit, so you hold him off.

"Now it's my turn!" you pant, staring into his eyes and grinding your groin into his, the feel of his hardness against you so satisfying that you have to force yourself to stop. You know if you rub against him even a little longer, even though he's still in his jeans and he's barely touched you, you'll come in seconds. But you don't want to come yet—you have other plans. He lifts his head and tries to kiss you, but you only let him for a second before you pull your head up. You're in charge now.

Still straddling him, your knees cushioned by the shag of the carpet, you let go of his wrists and tear his

T-shirt off over his head. Then you crawl down the length of him, nibbling on his muscled chest, taking each of his nipples between your teeth briefly and hearing him groan with pleasure. Then you pop open the button of his jeans, pull down the zipper, and tug them down and off his legs, releasing the biggest, hardest cock you've ever seen. He's so big you're a little scared at the thought of having him inside you. He cranes his head up, and a proud smile creeps across his face.

"Lie still!" you purr as you reach for the bottle of tequila and pour a shot into his navel. It overflows, and you watch as tequila runs across his skin in all directions, some down toward his crotch, running in small rivulets through his black pubic hair.

You kneel next to him and hold up the saltshaker. He looks at you expectantly, and you bend down and take his cock in one hand, then lick it slowly from the base all the way up to the tip, cupping and gently squeezing his balls in your other hand. Then you run your tongue back down the length of his cock. He closes his eyes and throws his head back, moaning with pleasure, and now he's the one struggling not to spill the tequila in his navel.

It's your turn to have him at your mercy, and you're loving every second of it. You shove a piece of orange in his mouth, which muffles his groans. Then you pour a small line of salt along the line you licked and slowly tongue the grains off his cock, feeling it pulsing under your tongue. Then you suck the tequila out of his belly button, licking around it to get every last drop. You straddle him again and crawl up the length of him to bite down on the orange gripped between his teeth, relishing the taste of citrus chasing the tequila down your throat.

Unable to hold off any longer, Charlie rolls you off him and on to your back, holding your arms against the shag carpet and grinding his cock against you.

"I want you inside me," you pant, unable to bear the suspense any longer. You feel him pulling off your purple lace G-string, and you're momentarily grateful that it's what you went for instead of the granny panties or the support Lycra. And then you feel the head of his cock up against you.

"Gently," you whisper, and "carefully," sitting up a little, suddenly concerned about protection.

He nods at you, understanding, and reaches for a condom in the pocket of his jeans, which are lying in a heap beside you. You lie back, excited, your breath coming fast. Then he raises himself up on one arm and rolls it on to his cock.

"Gently!" you whisper again, throwing your head back and opening your legs wider for him.

Slowly he pushes his cock inside you. You're so wet that the head of his cock slips into you easily, but then you feel your pussy stretch as you take in more and more of him, and you arch your back as he fills you completely and entirely. It's insanely pleasurable, especially as his strokes, gentle at first, become harder and faster—he's bordering on being too big for you, but the sensation is so good you don't want to stop him.

Just as he's building up a rhythm, he slips out of you briefly and you take the opportunity to turn over onto your stomach. You kneel and raise your bottom in the air and he groans with desire as he comes at you from behind, entering you again. You can feel the top of his cock pushing against the G-spot deep inside you, and you know that's what you wanted to feel, and your knees begin to shake as, with every single hard thrust, he takes you closer and closer to a wild orgasm. And soon he's holding on to your hips and slamming into you and you can't hold back anymore, so you push back against him, controlling the depth of every thrust just the way you want it, until it takes just one more thrust, just one more, to make you go over the edge and your eyes roll back in your head, and your toes curl and your pussy contracts a million times as you both come at the same time, you with a long guttural moan and him with a shout as he squeezes your hips, and then slaps your bottom with an enormous hand, the delicious sting of the slap extending your orgasm, heightening the intensity of it.

Eventually, just when you think your shaking legs can't hold you up any longer, he eases himself out of you and you collapse on your side on the carpet, your body slick with sweat. Charlie flops down next to you and pulls you toward him, your back against his stomach. You feel entirely satisfied, your head light with tequila and pleasure, your legs entwined as your body convulses with a series of aftershocks, his arms wrapped around you.

When you finally open your eyes again a hundred

Helena S. Paige

years later, you trace the scrawl of the tattoo down the length of his right arm, the one you didn't lick—yet. It reads: *I don't know where I'm going from here, but I promise it won't be boring.* You smile as you feel him getting hard again, that giant cock beginning to stir against your back.

"You know what we should do?" he says, drumming lightly up the side of your arm with his fingertips.

"What?" What on earth could he want now? you wonder. "How can you possibly be ready to go again?" you ask, astonished by his stamina.

He grins and shrugs, but his eyes flick to a small plastic packet that must have fallen out of his pocket when he pulled out the condom. There are several blue pills inside it. You know exactly what they are; you get spam about them in your email inbox all the time. He clears his throat and pushes his jeans on top of the telltale packet.

You feel a little disappointed: a rock star who has to take Viagra? Hardly the mental picture you had of this guy.

"Do you want to do something a little wild?" he asks.

"Wild?" you ask nervously.

"Yeah," he says, giving you a squeeze, "something a little different, a little . . . you know . . . kinky!"

"Depends on what you have in mind." You're a bit worried about what kind of depraved monkey sex this guy is planning next. If he thinks that monstrous organ is going anywhere near your other orifices, he's got another think coming.

"Well, I thought maybe we could take a shower together," he says. "The shower in this suite is completely insane; it has a killer view of the city."

❧ If you decide to take a shower with a rock star, go to page 37.

❧ If you're tired and ready to go home, go to page 42.

❧ You've decided to take a shower with a rock star

 You exhale. Phew, just sex in the shower. That's not all that kinky. Viagra or no Viagra, you can easily do that with a hot rock star, in a luxury hotel bathroom with a breathtaking view. Plus it's been a long, steamy night, so the thought of cool water sounds tempting. You imagine those big hands lathering soap over your body and you start to get wet all over again.

"That sounds great," you say, turning your head and kissing the underside of his jawline, and then running your mouth up the side of his neck. He cups one of your breasts and rolls the nipple between two fingers; your body is still sensitive after your enormous orgasm, so it's delightful agony.

He gets up and reaches for your hand. "Come on, then, let's go."

You let him pull you up. Then you follow him to the

master suite. The massive picture window looks out over the jewel box of lights that is the city, and there's a giant circular bed in the middle of the room.

He tugs at your hand and you follow him into the bathroom, which is almost bigger than your entire apartment. The floor is made of huge slabs of marble, and the lights of the cityscape glimmer through another floor-to-ceiling window.

Still holding your hand, Charlie opens the shower door and steps in, leading you behind him. There's plenty of space for both of you, and there's even a marble ledge in case you want to sit down to admire the view of the city and the night sky.

He turns on the taps and you feel the pressure of the water coming at you from a dozen different jets at various heights and angles, pure heaven on your still-heated body. He pulls you toward him and kisses you deeply as the water rains down on you. Your knees are still slightly shaky from your earlier orgasm, and as you feel him stroking a silky bar of soap up and down your back, you lean in to him. The soap slips between your ass cheeks and then down to your pussy, which is throbbing again in response to his touch.

"Oh my god," you groan, the pleasure of it making you weak at the knees.

He looks down at you, and you notice that his wet hair is plastered to his forehead, which makes him look a little goofy. You also register that he must have been wearing mascara, and it's clearly not the waterproof type, because it's smudged below his eyes. You step back and watch in dismay as the David Bowie quote on his arm starts to bleed and seep, the pen lines dissolving under the assault of the water.

"Baby," he says, his face earnest.

You nod, not sure you can speak.

"Will you do something for me?" he asks.

A little prickle of worry creeps up your spine.

"There's something I like—you may think it's a little strange, but I find it really hot," he says. "And if you give it a chance, I'm hoping you might like it, too."

You clear your throat: "Yes?" How bad can it be? you wonder. Even if he wears makeup and needs Viagra, and his tattoos aren't all real, he's still the drummer for the Space Cowboys, he's still pretty damn hot, and the sex earlier was incredible. Whatever he's about to ask you to do, you're fairly sure you can do it. At the very least, you'll consider it with an open mind.

He holds you by the wrists, looks into your eyes almost pleadingly. Then he says: "I really want you to pee on me."

You suck in your breath, concentrating hard on not pulling a face. Open mind, open mind, open mind, you repeat silently to yourself.

"What?" Maybe, if you're lucky, you misheard him.

"It would really, seriously, totally turn me on if you would pee on me," he repeats, looking hopeful.

"Um . . ." you say. "You want me to pee? On your body?" You thought that was something people only did if they'd been stung by jellyfish.

He nods and smiles that sexy smile of his. But he

a girl walks into a bar

39

doesn't look quite so sexy anymore, with raccoon eyes and flat hair that's revealing a bit of a thinning spot now that the gel has washed out. "Yes," he says. "It's really hot. I'll sit down on the ledge, and we'll turn off the taps, and then you can just pee on me, wherever you want; go wild."

"Ummmm." You hesitate. "Umm, I don't really have to go right now, but let me drink some water and get us each a glass of champagne, and then I'm sure I'll be able to deliver. How does that sound? Okay?"

His eyes light up at your reaction. "Awesome!" he shrieks. "Jesus, you're amazing, this is going to be so hot!"

You smile and kiss him lightly on the lips, then step out of the shower. "You wait here, you sexy beast, I'll be right back."

As you tiptoe out of the bathroom, taking care not to slip on the marble floor, you look back to see him playing air guitar in the shower.

You hurry into the sitting room, water still dripping off your naked body. You grab a throw off the couch—it looks expensive, but who cares?—and blot at yourself. You scoop your underwear off the floor, and tug your dress on over your damp skin. Then you grab your shoes and your handbag and tiptoe out the door of the suite, closing it quietly behind you. You bolt to the elevator, laughing hysterically as you picture Charlie turning into a prune in the shower—and his face when he realizes that you're not coming back.

It's definitely time to head home to a DVD and a big

bowl of popcorn. Or wait: maybe you should drop in on Melissa—she's never going to believe this!

- 🔖 To go straight home, go to page 217.

- 🔖 If you want to swing past Melissa's place on your way home to tell her about your crazy night, go to page 249.

a girl walks into a bar

❧ You're tired and you just want to go home

You YAWN AND STRETCH. You're tired and sated. Behind you, Charlie's hardening cock presses into your back. You feel like you're in some kind of dream, where normal girls fuck hot rock stars on shag rugs in expensive hotel suites overlooking the city. You think if someone were to pinch you right now, you'd probably wake up and everything would all be over.

The perfect ending to the perfect night would be if you could curl up and sleep for hours, but if the truncheon prodding you in the small of your back, and that bag full of Viagra are anything to go by, this guy's still got a couple of rounds left in him. After all that champagne and tequila, followed by great, pounding sex, you don't think you're up for any more. The thought of that enormous cock inside you again is tempting, but too exhausting to contemplate. And anyway, a rock star who needs to take Viagra—isn't that a bit lame?

"You know what?" you say, turning to face him.

"What?" he says, grinning confidently.

"I've had the most incredible evening, but I think I'm going to call it a night." You kiss him hard on the lips, then jump up and reach for your dress before he can pull you back down again. "Thank you for everything."

He looks at you in disbelief. "You mean you're not going to stay?"

You shake your head and he watches, dumbfounded, as you slip into your dress, locate your shoes, and stuff your purple G-string and bra into your handbag.

"Maybe we can do this again sometime?" he asks, his voice almost bordering on pleading.

"Maybe." You smile mysteriously as you head for the door.

On the way down in the elevator, you almost have to pinch yourself. Definitely time to go home. Or maybe you could go via your local late-night coffee shop and pick up a hot chocolate on the way?

❧ If you go straight home, go to page 217.

❧ If you swing by the coffee shop on the way home, go to page 242.

❧ If you're not quite ready to go home yet, go to page 240.

a girl walks into a bar

❧ You've decided you don't want to drink tequila
with a rock star

 You eye the tequila shot in front of you, and
the smell makes you queasy. You just don't think it's a
good idea. Charlie looks at you expectantly, and in that
moment a rogue thought runs through your mind: you
think of all the women he must have screwed. You'd just
be another number, another conquest, and the arrogant
ass hasn't even bothered to ask your name yet—that's
how confident he is. Nah, you think, he's actually a bit of
a tool. Enormous hands or not, there's nothing less sexy
than overconfidence.

"Thank you," you say, slipping off your bar stool, "but
another time, perhaps."

"You're going?" he asks, his jaw dropping.

You nod and wonder if this is the first time a woman

has ever turned him down; he clearly doesn't know how to react.

You leave him seated at the bar, and as you reach the door, you look back to see that he's already chatting up two blonde girls, offering them the remaining tequila shots. You smile, pleased with your decision as you step out of the bar into the cool, clear night.

But now what to do? You wish Mr. Intense hadn't gone back to his business meeting—there was something magnetic about him. And that intriguing woman in the ladies' room—it might be fun to have a drink with her. Perhaps you should head to the exhibition and see if she's there?

Maybe it's time to call a taxi—the night is still young.

Or you could just head home to entertain yourself. You visualize the box in the drawer next to your bedside table. It was a gift from two girlfriends for your last birthday. In it there's a vibrator, still nestled neatly in its packaging. It's called a Bunny—no, wait, a Rabbit. It was supposed to be a joke, but you all knew it wasn't *actually* a joke. You've been so busy building your career over the last couple of years that your friends have started worrying a little about the drought you're in.

You've never even used it yet, but maybe tonight is the night. That way at least, you'd be guaranteed a happy ending.

❧ If it's not time to go home yet, but you're not in the mood for an art exhibition, go to page 47.

a girl walks into a bar

❧ If you want to get to the exhibition before it closes, go to page 52.

❧ If you want to head straight home to your Rabbit, go to page 253.

Helena L. Paige

~ You've decided to call a taxi

 You look at your watch again. It's been fifteen minutes since you called for a taxi, and you're starting to get annoyed. They said five minutes, but this is beginning to feel like the longest five minutes in history. A couple of giggling women in platform heels exit the bar and totter past you, arm in arm. You reach into your handbag for your phone, and your eye catches the flyer you were given earlier. You fish it out and examine it again: the intriguing name "Immaculata" printed over the shot of the woman with enticing eyes you met in the bathroom. You scan the address. You know where that is; it's only a couple of blocks from here. You could walk it, even in these heels.

Two guys whistle at you from across the street. "All right, darlin'?" one of them yells, clutching his crotch. "If I could see you naked, I'd die happy."

After Chest Wig's unwanted attention earlier this evening, you're not in the mood to take anymore bullshit. "Yeah?" you call back. "If I could see you naked, I'd die laughing."

You're surprised when they duck their heads and scurry away. Your comeback wasn't *that* sharp.

"Everything okay?"

You look up to see the tree trunk of a man with the deep voice. The bodyguard for the Space Cowboys. That probably explains why those idiots looked so sheepish.

"Hi," you say. "I'm just waiting for my taxi. They said five minutes, but taxi companies have a different understanding of time than the rest of us."

He laughs and sits down next to you on the metal railing that runs along the wall outside the bar.

"So you decided not to party with Charlie, then?" he asks.

"He didn't send you out here to drag me back in there, did he?"

"No way. He doesn't pay me enough to do that kind of work."

"Yeah, you know, it was fun and all, but he's not really my type."

"Well, he is my boss, but between you and me, you made a good call."

"I think so, too," you say. "Thanks for the vote of confidence."

"Can I offer you a lift home?" he asks, stepping toward the curb.

"Won't you be missed inside?"

"Nah, I've been sent on a run," he says. "I can take

48

you anywhere you want to go. They won't miss me for a while."

"A run?"

"You know, a run."

"Like for drugs or something?"

"Do I look like the kind of guy who'd do something like that?"

"Well . . ."

"Seriously, it's nothing illegal. You can trust me. I'm an ex-cop."

"I'm guessing that running after rock stars is more lucrative than rounding up drunks or solving murders."

He shrugs. "This job has its perks." He points a remote toward the curb and presses a button. You watch as the lights on a sleek black sports car flash in response. Your jaw drops, and he grins at your reaction.

The car sits low to the ground, its mag wheels and custom paint job catching the light from the bar's neon sign. "Is that a 350Z?" you ask.

He nods approvingly. "You know your cars."

"It's the Gran Turismo special-edition model, isn't it? Didn't they only make a few hundred of them?"

"How the hell would you know that?" he asks, looking at you in admiration. "But yeah, you're spot-on."

"Isn't it the one with the additional horsepower?"

Now he's really floored. This is fun, you think, trying to dredge up more car facts. No need to tell him that you only recognize it because one of your exes was a *Top Gear* fanatic who subjected you to thousands of hours of sports-car porn.

"Wish it was mine," he says. "But luckily for me, Charlie is usually too wasted to drive it, so I get a lot of time behind the wheel." His phone rings, and his hand darts into his pocket to retrieve it. "I have to take this. Won't be a minute. After that, I can take you wherever you need to go." He walks over to the corner so that he can take the call in privacy.

You picture yourself tearing through the late-night streets with him in that gorgeous car. And, the car aside, he's not at all bad-looking. Even though he's huge, he clearly works out, and you suspect every inch of that body is pure muscle.

A taxi pulls up in front of you, interrupting your thoughts, and the driver gets out and leans over the roof of the car.

"Finally! That must have been the world's longest five minutes!" you say to him, hands on your hips.

He looks at a piece of paper he's holding, his face confused. "Mr. Cornetto?" he asks.

"No!" you snap. "I called you almost half an hour ago. Your guy said you'd be five minutes!"

"I'm afraid this taxi is for a Mr. Cornetto."

"I think you must mean me," says a voice from behind. You whirl around, ready to confront whoever is trying to steal your taxi, and you're taken aback when you see the sexy salt-and-pepper guy who rescued you from Chest Wig earlier. Mr. Intense. The guy who smells like a blend of cedar and leather. The one who could give George Clooney a run for his money. Miles, was it?

"Oh, it's you," you say. Then redden with embarrassment. At this rate, you're going to slay him with your wit.

"Is everything all right?" he asks, looking from you to the taxi driver.

"Everything's fine. I was just waiting for a taxi, but this isn't it."

"Well, there's no reason it couldn't be," he says. "Why don't we share it?"

"No, I wouldn't want to impose—it's fine, really. He offered me a ride, too," you say, indicating the bodyguard on the corner, who's having some kind of altercation with whoever's on the phone. "And anyway, you already helped me out once tonight."

"Are you sure? Your friend looks like he's got his hands full."

He's so attractive that you struggle not to stare. Dropping your head, you notice you're still clutching the "Immaculata" invitation. Your thoughts buzz as you try to decide what to do next.

✎ If you go to the art exhibition, go to page 52.

✎ If you share a taxi with the George Clooney look-alike, go to page 105.

✎ If you take a ride home in the sports car with the bodyguard, go to page 162.

❧ You've decided to check out the exhibition at
the gallery

AT THE ENTRANCE TO the gallery, the image from
the flyer stares down at you from an enormous poster, the
word "Immaculata" splashed across it. You're definitely
in the right place.

You walk into the viewing space, and are struck by
the low, intimate lighting, the only bright spotlights reserved for the vivid images hung around the room. The
area isn't packed, but it's busy enough, with small clusters
of people dotted around the space, chatting, drinking
sparkling wine, and taking in the art.

You wander over to the first piece of work. It's a
modern-day photographic version of those lush flower
paintings by Georgia O'Keeffe, the ones that look like
vaginas. This fleshy rose-colored bloom really does re-
semble the real deal. You peer more closely and almost
squeak out loud: you're not looking at a flower but at an

actual vagina—or rather, into one. You glance around to see if anyone else has noticed and is as taken aback as you are, then crane forward again, fascinated in spite of yourself. Yup, that's a pussy right there up on the wall.

Maybe you've got it wrong. Maybe you have a dirty mind. You move hastily to the next picture. Oh my god. This time it's a shot of a woman's naked pelvis, from the waist to the thighs. The subject is sitting back, relaxed, legs half open, a thick and lustrous black bush between them, one hand trailing casually across her inner thigh. You gulp, but can't help noticing that the pose looks natural and powerful.

The next few photos, all color-saturated so that the skin glows, are variations on this theme: in some, the focus is so close that you can see the grain in the skin, the fine hairs on the belly; in others, the focus is blurred so that the pussy shots really do look like Impressionist roses and lilies, in every shade of scarlet, pink, mocha, and maroon.

Finally you come to a larger picture. This shot shows most of the woman's lower body as she lies back on a rumpled bed, her legs apart and her pussy rosy in a nest of thick, dark hair. The faintly curving tummy and one breast, nipple on the alert, stretch away into the background. It's not at all pornographic, though. There's something intimate, almost reverent in the way her body is presented.

You put your hand on your throat and are surprised to find you're sweating lightly.

You're still staring when a hand slides lightly down

a girl walks into a bar

your arm. "Enjoying the show?" a voice says huskily in your ear. It's the woman from the bathroom in the bar, whose face is on the posters.

"Oh, hello! Um, yes, very original," you manage. "Are you the artist? I mean, the photographer? Did you have trouble getting the models . . . to pose?" You know you sound like a babbling idiot, but this woman unnerves you.

She laughs, a smoky, furred sound. "Not really. In fact, rumor has it this model was a pleasure to work with."

You're confused. She puts her hand on the small of your back and turns you toward a photo in the corner. You stare in amazement: it's her. And in the photo, she's stark naked, and everything, and it really is everything, is on display. The woman in the photograph gazes proudly out at the viewer, her neck held erect, her gravity-defying breasts decorated only by an ornate silver cross that dangles between them. She's sitting on a sofa, one leg relaxed, the other dangling over the arm of the couch.

You're completely tongue-tied. You flounder a bit and eventually come out with "Are you Immaculata?"

"That's what my mother named me. My friends call me Mac, though."

You turn to look at her—anything to drag your eyes away from the photo on the wall—and you notice that her chandelier earrings have little silver-and-jet skulls dangling from them.

"So, what do you think?" she asks, drawing your

Helena L. Paige

54

attention back to the incredibly intimate photographs, some of them more than six feet high.

"They're—they're—quite something," you stammer. "I've never seen anything quite like them."

"Thank you," she says simply. "I like them, too."

"I think it's really brave of you to expose yourself like that. I don't know if I'd have the guts."

"Why not?" she asks, turning toward you. When she focuses on you, it's as if there's no one else in the room.

"I don't know. It's so . . . so . . . intimate, I suppose."

"Intimate, yes," she says, "but also liberating. It was a real rush, to tell the truth."

"You didn't feel shy or embarrassed?"

"Not at all. And Cat made it easy."

"Cat?"

"The photographer. She works with Jan Kollwitz. He's the famous one, but he says that in a few years' time she'll be serious competition." She's talking as if you should know exactly who she means, and the Jan guy's name does ring a vague bell.

"They're around here somewhere. Oh look, speak of the devils!" Mac raises a graceful arm and signals at a couple across the room. The woman is surrounded by congratulatory folk and is accepting compliments and an endless series of cheek kisses, while the guy is hanging back, smiling proudly. He's not conventionally handsome, with that craggy profile and those deep-set eyes. But he's definitely attractive in that antihero sort of way. He's casually dressed in blue jeans and a gray sweater with a crew neck. She's younger, her shining hair cut into slanted wings, and she's simply dressed in a pearl-gray silk shift over narrow black jeans, with flat paisley pumps. She keeps turning to her partner, laughing up at him and nudging his arm.

"They make a good couple," you say, and Mac gives her throaty laugh again.

"Oh, that's funny! But it's a mistake a lot of people make."

You're even more confused. "Why is it funny?"

"Cat is gay and Jan is very, very hetero. In any case, he's her supervisor. He's been mentoring her for a while now; she works on a lot of his shoots. This is her degree exhibition for her masters in fine arts."

You barely have time to rearrange your mental furniture before Cat comes over, Jan following her.

"Oh, thank god for you," Cat says, hugging Mac. "I thought I was never going to get out of that conversation!"

"Congratulations on the show," you say.

She grins. "My examiners are either going to have collective heart attacks or give me top marks. We're not sure which way it's going to go yet."

Mac smiles again, that suggestive beauty spot on her cheek tugging upward. "My friend here was asking how it felt to expose myself. Me, I recommend it."

"Well, it helps that you're a natural exhibitionist, being a dancer," Cat teases. She turns to you. "Mac's an old friend. I wanted to do something experimental, and this is an idea we've been batting around for a while. And she was willing to let it all, er, hang out. But

Jan is really the expert here at photographing women's bodies."

"You're exaggerating," Jan says, looking slightly abashed. You like him for it.

Cat turns to you. "If you're interested, you should give it a try."

Mac smiles, teasing and challenging: "You never know, you might get a thrill out of it."

You shake your head instinctively.

"Don't tell me you're not a little tempted?" Mac says.

"Seriously," Cat interjects thoughtfully, "I think you'd really work well as a subject." The three of them focus on you, and your stomach flips.

"Jan, wouldn't she be perfect for that black-and-white series you're doing? Look at the texture of her skin!" says Cat.

"Hello, people, I'm right here," you say, flustered but also flattered.

Cat laughs. "Listen, I have to go and circulate, people to see, funders to schmooze. Mac, please come and prop me up. I need the moral support. Jan, why don't you tell this lovely girl more about your project?" She heads off, summoned by a small gang of enthusiastic admirers.

Mac reaches for your wrist, her fingers cool on your skin: "You really should think about it, *chica*. It would be good to see . . . more of you." Then she glides after Cat.

There's a pause, and Jan seems in no hurry to break the silence. Instead, his eyes travel slowly over your face and body, as if he's committing you to memory. You start to feel self-conscious, but at the same time, there's something oddly exciting about being the object of such intense scrutiny. The seconds drag by, and you search for something to say.

But before you can speak, he says, as if reaching a decision, "Cat's right. You *would* make a good subject. The way your neck curves, flows into your shoulder . . ." He takes another long look at you. "So do you think you'd be interested?"

"Oh, no, I don't really . . . I mean I couldn't . . ."

"Because if you were, I'd really like to shoot you."

"You would?"

"Of course. Not exactly like this, of course," he says, gesturing at the collection of lush nudes hanging on the walls. "This is very much Cat's style. I'm busy with a series that has some similarities, I suppose, but the feel, the textures are different. It's a study of different parts of the body."

"Oh?"

"Like the neck, for example."

"The neck?" you parrot, stroking yours and then feeling a little foolish.

"For me, there's something more deeply suggestive when you go beyond the obviously erotic parts of the body. The line of the neck, the inside of an elbow or the dips between barefoot toes—those can be way more sensual than the sexual organs themselves. You know what I mean?"

You half nod.

"Maybe it's something about the curve of the collar-bone, or the tension of the calf. And all those parts of the body where the skin hardly ever gets touched. The parts that are the last places to see the sun. That's where the skin is softest. Like here," he says, reaching for your hand and turning your arm over. He runs his thumb across the soft inner skin in the crook of your elbow, making you shiver. "That's what fascinates me." His slightly gravelly voice tapers off.

He shakes his head, snapping out of it, as if hearing himself for the first time. "Sorry," he says, with a self-deprecating smile that takes you off guard. It instantly transforms him from an intense artist into someone much more approachable. "I get carried away sometimes. That must have come across as a lot of pretentious crap. The truth is, I'm better behind the camera."

"No, it's actually quite interesting. I'd never thought of it that way." He's right, there is something erotic about those neglected parts of the body.

"So what do you say? Would you allow me to take some shots?"

You shake your head instinctively. "Oh, I don't know. I mean, I'm not sure . . ."

"They wouldn't be nude shots; you'd be wearing a robe. And I'd only be shooting you from here." He indicates from his chest upward. "And maybe an arm, or the back of your leg, if you're willing."

You clear your throat, intrigued and flattered by the idea of being photographed by this man. It might be fun, as long as nobody ever knew it was you. And if you didn't have to get entirely naked, it wouldn't be too embarrassing, would it? It's not every day a famous profes-

sional offers to take your photograph. You could always ask Melissa to come along with you. She'd think it was hilarious. Or you could always politely bow out if you changed your mind.

"Sure, why not?"

"Excellent!" he says. "This is going to be great. Let's get out of here."

"What, *now*?" Your voice comes out as a squeak.

"Why not? I'd love to escape. There's an art critic hovering over there who's been dying to bore me to death all night."

"Hold on a second. How do I know you aren't a serial killer who's going to post pictures of my dismembered body all over Facebook? Where are you taking me?"

He laughs. "We can ask Cat to come along once she's finished circulating, if that would make you feel more comfortable. Besides, I need her help cutting up the bodies."

He relents at the expression on your face, pulls out his wallet, and hands you a business card. Beneath the name "Kollwitz" and a cell-phone number, there's a studio address. If you're not mistaken, it's just around the corner.

You flip the card over and on the back there's an image of Angel Dean's face. You recognize it—a black-and-white version of the one on the cover of *Cosmo* a couple of months ago.

"You took this?"

A nod.

Helena L. Paige

"You're kidding. But if this is your average model, why on earth would you want to photograph *me*?"

"Why on earth wouldn't I?" he says.

You stare at him, your mind racing. Should you take him up on his offer? You scan the gallery for Mac and Cat. Maybe you should just stay here for a little longer, take a look at the rest of the photographs. Then again, this is all rather unfamiliar territory for you. Perhaps you should go back to the bar for one last drink (and another look at that very cute bartender).

❧ If you decide to go off with the photographer, go to page 62.

❧ If you decide to turn down his offer and stay at the gallery, go to page 85.

❧ If you decide to head back to the bar, go to page 186.

a girl walks into a bar

❧ You've decided to go with the photographer

You WAIT JUST INSIDE the entrance to the studio, in the dark, while Jan turns off the alarm system and flicks on a couple of lights. Your heart's thumping the beat of a frenetic house track. He's not a complete stranger, you tell yourself. There is no way he's a real, live serial killer. He's a famous professional photographer, and he's shot Angel Dean, for heaven's sake. And you know for a fact that she's still alive. Thin, but alive.

The rest of the lights stutter on, revealing a huge open-plan area with high ceilings. Off to one side are retro leather-and-wood chairs and a settee. The armchairs are solid, 1960s-style, with armrests that curl into small built-in side tables.

The studio also contains several small rooms off to the back, with what looks like an office, a kitchenette, a bathroom, and a darkroom. One entire wall is a white infinity curve stretching up to the ceiling.

As you prowl around, you spot a Harley-Davidson vintage chopper parked in a shadowy corner. All black and chrome, more worn than shiny.

You point to the bike. "Is that yours? It's gorgeous."

Jan looks up from where he's busy at a counter covered with photographic equipment: light meters, lenses, plugs, cables, and memory cards, along with several cameras. "It's just a prop," he says.

You keep wandering around the studio, trying to take your mind off what's ahead. You come across a desk with stacks of photographs and contact sheets piled on it. You flick through a couple. They show a group of huge, tattooed Hells Angels surrounding a tall, beautiful woman who's lounging on the bike. The same bike you were just admiring. She looks familiar. Very familiar . . . "Holy smoke!" you blurt out. "Is that Alex Khan?"

"Yes. It's for the cover of *The Face*." He doesn't sound like he's bragging. "They're okay, but if I could do that shoot again, there are a few things I would do differently."

"Wow. What's she like?"

"She's a dream to work with. A real pro."

You nod, your heart still beating a mile a minute. A real pro. Of course she is. And here's you. Who is most assuredly not a pro. What have you gotten yourself into? How can you live up to Alex Khan? Next he'll be telling you he's best friends with Anna Wintour.

a girl walks into a bar

Jan flicks a remote, and a mellow but funky track fills the studio.

"Wine?" he asks.

"Oh god, yes please."

He disappears into the kitchen, and you hear a cork pop. Seconds later he's back, carrying two half-full glasses of red wine.

You tap glasses and take a sip. It's good. Tastes expensive.

He steps over to his workstation and selects a bulky camera that looks old-fashioned, especially compared to all the technology surrounding it.

"I was thinking we should go old-school," he says. "Forget digital, I'm talking real film. Black and white. Large format."

You take another gulp of wine. "So how does this work?"

"Well, there are a couple of robes in the cupboard in the bathroom, if you still want to do this. Of course, we don't have to shoot anything you're not comfortable with."

You chew a finger, hesitating. This is your chance to be photographed by someone who's shot some of the most spectacular models in the world. But you're no model—maybe you should head back to the gallery and tell Mac you're not cut out to be a photographer's muse. Or perhaps, after all this excitement, you need a quiet drink back at the bar.

❧ If you stick around and go for it, go to page 66.

❧ If you decide this is not for you and head back to the gallery, go to page 85.

❧ If you go back to the bar, go to page 186.

a girl walks into a bar

❧ You stick around and go for it

🍸 LIKE THE REST OF the studio, the bathroom is spacious and beautifully styled. There's a leather chaise longue against one wall, as well as a shower, a toilet, a sink, and a retro cabinet. An elegant black chandelier hangs from the ceiling, the only non-white object in the room. You've always wanted a chandelier in your bathroom.

Inside the cabinet you find towels and a couple of folded white robes. You pull one out, and when you hold it to your nose the immensely soft fabric smells fresh and clean, with a hint of the ocean.

You pull your dress off over your head and unclasp your bra. Then you face the mirror and cover your breasts with both arms, trying to decide how you feel about this. And you realize that you're not only nervous and excited, but a little turned on. The thought of being photographed like this by a near-stranger is strangely sexy. Maybe it's because it's so completely out of character for you that the thought of it is so racy, so daring. Plus the guy has shot some of the most iconic women in the world. You cannot wait to tell Melissa about this.

You take a deep breath. Then you assess your body in the mirror again, trying to look past the flaws you see in yourself. You remember that what made the photos of Mac so erotic was her sheer confidence, the way she opened her whole self to the camera.

Emboldened, you slip off your purple lacy G-string and slip the robe on over your shoulders, the fabric so light it feels like it's barely there. Jan doesn't need to know that you're entirely naked under it. You like the idea of having a little secret. You tie the belt loosely around your waist, then glance down at your stiletto heels, deciding that they will be the only things you leave on.

Back in the studio, Jan has set up a couple of lights on the infinity curve and is busy adjusting the camera with long, ringed fingers. You walk over to him slowly, feeling jittery. This must be what second thoughts feel like.

Jan looks up and smiles warmly at you. "I'll be ready in a second. Make yourself comfortable."

You approach the black leather bar stool he's placed in the middle of the infinity curve and hover for a second before climbing on, pulling the robe down over your knees and clutching it closed at your chest.

Once he's ready, Jan walks over to you. "I thought

we'd just start with a couple of photos of your neck, from here to here." He indicates the area between the top of his chest and his chin.

You nod, trying to act professional.

Jan gives you a few quiet instructions and helps you settle into place, your neck extended as far as it will go and your chin jutting out at what feels like an awkward angle, although he assures you that the camera reads it as normal.

He takes little steps, moving around you like a hairdresser, clicking off a couple of shots on a digital camera first, so he can see how the lighting's working.

"Here, take a look. What do you think?" he says, bending down beside you and scrolling through some of the shots. They're all in black and white, most of them super close-up. There are a few that make you gulp a bit, but on the whole you can't believe how artful they are. There's the curve of your clavicle in one, the round hill of your shoulder in another. He's right, even the underside of a chin can be sexy if it's framed and shot in a certain way.

His body brushes against yours and your thoughts scatter. Fortunately he's so focused on his work that he doesn't seem to notice the effect he's having on you. Perhaps it's the secret fact that you're naked under your robe that's making you a little hot and wet. You squeeze your knees together to hide the fact that they're shaking slightly.

In the pictures you've seen so far, the collar of your robe is showing on your shoulders, so you hold it chastely

Helena L. Paige

closed between your breasts, then let it slip off your shoulders a little so that it won't appear in the shots.

Jan snaps off a couple more pictures with the digital camera and then makes some adjustments to the lighting. You watch him moving around the studio, deft and quick. The photographer is focused, you think, stifling a giggle.

When he's finally satisfied, he changes over to the old-fashioned camera, and you go into serious pose mode. Keeping your knees together, you hook your heels on the bottom rung of the stool. Every time he shoots a picture, you hear the light popping and the click of the camera. It's warm under the lights, but pleasantly so, and after the first few shots you settle into your role as model, taking his direction, turning your neck farther to one side, shifting the angle of your chin. The camera acts as a barrier, and it feels less like he's staring at you, more like he's capturing you. With the mellow background music and the pop of the lights, it's easy to relax, and you begin to feel more comfortable in your own skin.

Plus there's something exciting about being the focus of such obvious skill. His attention is intimate yet distant at the same time.

At one point, Jan stops what he's doing and holds the camera away from himself, scrutinizing you. Then he comes over and strokes your hair away from your face. You sit up straighter and hold your breath as he touches you. As his fingers graze the side of your face, your nipples harden. You press your thighs together again,

a girl walks into a bar

feeling your pussy moisten. You can't help wondering if he had the same effect on Alex Khan and Angel Dean.

Then he steps back and raises the camera again. With a sudden rush of courage, you let go of the robe and drop your arms to your sides. The fabric falls away from you, taking the loosely tied belt with it, and you feel it skim your skin as it flutters to the ground and pools at your feet. On the way down, it brushes your nipples, making them even harder.

Jan continues shooting as if nothing has changed, although the blood is rushing through your ears so loudly, you doubt you'd hear anything he might say. Growing bolder, you shift position, parting your legs, but with both hands placed on the front of the stool, shielding yourself from the eye of the camera.

The lights carry on flaring with every shot. You swallow hard, take a deep breath and remove your hands. You place them behind you and arch your back, leaving yourself completely bared to him. You're sure the camera can see how wet you are. And the thought of it makes you even wetter.

You have no idea how long you remain there like that, shifting by degrees into minutely different poses. Time stretches.

"THAT'S THE ROLL," JAN says, bending to collect the gown and hand it to you. You slip it back on and climb off the stool.

"We got some really fine shots," he says, looking pleased. "The camera loves you."

You're not sure how to respond. You have so much adrenaline pumping through your veins, you can't even speak.

"So, how was that for you?" he asks.

You struggle to get yourself under control. "Incredible," you manage.

"Not as bad as you thought?"

"Nowhere near."

"Would you like to see how they came out?"

"Sure, but how?"

"I've got a darkroom, so we can develop them right now. Unless you're in a hurry to get out of here?"

You think for a minute. Do you really want to see how the photos came out? You're momentarily seized with doubt and embarrassment. You can't believe how brazen you were, dropping your gown like that and flaunting your naked self. It might be better if you never saw the pictures. But the thought of going into a small darkroom with Jan is an enticing one.

Wait: the whole experience has been so unreal, you never actually thought about there being real, live, naked photographs of you, out there in the world. Oh god, what if people see them? You consider snatching the camera and dashing for the exit. Grand larceny is a bit extreme, though, as is the idea of making a getaway dressed only in a stolen gown and high heels. Surely if you're unhappy with the pictures, you could try to per-

a girl walks into a bar

suade Jan to give you the negatives, or, better still, shred them. He seems like a reasonable guy.

Maybe it's better to take a look at the pictures first and then figure out how to deal with the situation—or is ignorance bliss? In which case, perhaps you'd better get your clothes back on and go back to the gallery, where you can look to your heart's content, but not be seen. But what are you going to do about the head of steam you've built up? There's always your Rabbit vibrator waiting for you back at home . . .

❧ If you stay and see how the pictures turn out, go to page 73.

❧ If you head back to the exhibition, go to page 85.

❧ If you want to go home to your Rabbit, go to page 253.

Helena L. Paige

❧ You've decided to stay and see how the pictures
turn out

THE TINY DARKROOM AT the back of the studio
smells sharply of chemicals. Two of the walls have waist-
height countertops lined with developing equipment,
trays, and bottles. A wire is strung between two walls,
peppered with pegs for the newly developed prints.

You and Jan stand side by side as he handles big plastic bottles and containers with the confidence of long
familiarity, pouring different chemicals into a series of
three trays. If you compare his relaxed body language
now with his discomfort earlier on in the gallery, when
he was being forced to be social, it's like being with a
completely different man.

"Each tray is for a different step in the process," he explains. "The first one is the developer, this second one is
a stop bath, and the last one is the fixer. The whole trick
with photography is the lighting," he says as he works.

"When you're taking the shots, the lighting needs to be just right, and then when you're developing them, there can't be any light at all. If any light gets in while we're developing these negatives, it's a total disaster."

Finishing his prep, he reaches for the wall and flips a switch. Everything goes black, and then a safety light comes on, bathing the room in a soft red glow.

There's a large machine on the other side of the counter and you watch as he feeds the roll of negatives through it. Once the negative has been processed, he takes out a pack of photographic paper and carefully removes a sheet. His face is intent, and the red light gives him a mysterious quality.

There's no music in the vault-like room, and all you can hear is breathing. His is slow and steady, and yours is slightly faster.

Jan slides the sheet of photographic paper into the developer fluid, gently rocking the tray, tipping up first the one end and then the other. He constantly checks the giant digital clock on the wall, the fluorescent numbers flashing as the seconds tick by. He looks sideways at you and smiles.

"Look," he whispers.

You lean across him and stare into the tray as the image forms slowly on the page. You suck in your breath as you see it taking shape. It's an extreme close-up in black and white of one of your breasts. You recognize the small freckle to the right of your nipple, which is hard and pointed, the areola slightly goose-bumped.

Helena L. Paige

You feel both your nipples instantly mirroring the image on the page in front of you. You can't help yourself—you grab his arm and squeeze it.

"Oh my god," you say. "That's me."

He smiles again. "Beautiful, isn't it?"

When it's ready, he pulls the paper out of the developer fluid with a pair of tongs, and after letting it drip and drain for a couple of seconds, he slides it into the second tray, tipping that as well to ensure the page is evenly covered by the solution, always keeping one eye on the clock.

Finally he pulls the paper out of the last tray, washes the print, and then hangs it up on the wire, clipping both corners with pegs.

You can't take your eyes off the print. You've only ever seen your breasts in a mirror or looking down on them, never like this, in such artistic detail. It's slightly surreal, particularly bathed in the low, red light.

While you're still examining the first print, Jan prepares the next negative, and then repeats the process over the three trays. Again the only sound in the darkroom is the both of you breathing, and you might be imagining it, but you think his breath is coming a little faster.

When the second image reveals itself, you gasp. This time it's a close-up of your neck. Your collarbone sweeps across at an angle, and there's a small bead of sweat in the dip below it. Then your neck arches up, long and regal, with just the curve of your chin going off the edge of the print at the top.

a girl walks into a bar

"To me, this is the most sensual part of your body," he says, watching you watching the image take shape on the page in the tray.

You touch your neck, running your fingers over the hot, pulsing skin. "Really?"

"Absolutely," he says, placing a tentative hand on your chest, running his ringed thumb over the swell of your collarbone and into the dip beyond it. "Right here."

You drop your hands, letting the sides of your gown fall apart, so you're standing next to him in the red-dark in nothing but your heels and an open robe. With a dream-like motion, he runs his hand farther down and then sideways, gently brushing over one of your breasts, barely touching it.

"Shit, my print!" he says, glancing at the timer and whipping back to his trays. He shifts the almost over-exposed print to the next tray. Eventually, after rinsing, he clips it up beside the image of your breast.

"That was close," he says. He turns back to his work, and as much as you're disappointed that he's no longer touching you, you're keen to see how the rest of the pictures come out. He develops three or four more in quick succession. You watch in silence, fascinated by the process and the lottery of the images, never knowing which part of your body is going to appear out of the liquid next. The smell of the chemicals is overwhelming, but you're sure it's overpowered by the scent of your body.

There's an image of your ankle and the turn of your foot in its stiletto floating in the first tray, and another extreme close-up, this one of the nape of your neck, in

Helena L. Paige

the second tray. He slips it into the third tray and moves each picture along, one step in the system.

You're astonished by how sensual they are, even the ones of just a foot or an elbow.

And then he slips a piece of the paper into the first tray, and a picture of your pussy blooms slowly out of the liquid. Even in the safe light of the darkroom, you can see every intimate detail. It glistens, wet on the page.

You blurt out without thinking: "God, I'm wet!"

Jan abandons the prints swimming in the trays and grabs you, pushing you up against a wall. Your gown is still hanging open, and he snakes his arms around your waist, pulling you into him, hands warm on your back. You can feel him hard against you as he kisses you, his lips hot against yours and then his tongue eagerly exploring your mouth. You let your body crush into his, and run your fingers around the back of his head, up into his hair, gripping him closer.

Then he drops his hands down onto your bottom and lifts you up. You wrap your legs around him and refuse to stop kissing him. He carries you, turning a half-circle and putting you down on the countertop. Some of the bottles and other paraphernalia clatter to the floor, something smashes, but you carry on kissing, too far in now to want to stop.

He tilts your head back with one hand and starts kissing the length of your neck, using his teeth and his tongue, and you cry out as he takes both your breasts in his hands, your nipples between his fingers. You feel the steel of his ring on your nipple, and it makes you shiver.

a girl walks into a bar

He takes your arm and stretches it out in front of him. First he rubs his thumb over the soft inner skin, like he did earlier, but this time more intimately, and then he drops his mouth onto it and teases at the delicate skin, sending an electric jolt of pleasure through your body. Then he pushes you gently back against the wall and lifts your right leg, placing one stilettoed foot on the countertop, laying your pussy bare to him. He reaches behind you and pulls your bottom forward, so that your pelvis is as close to the edge of the counter as possible, your upper back and shoulders leaning against the wall.

Then he clasps your left leg and runs his thumb over the sensitive strip of skin at the back of your knee as he drops his mouth onto your pussy. You groan as he starts slowly licking your clit, then nudging it with his nose as he briefly dips his tongue inside you. He runs his mouth up and down the full length of your slit. As he reaches the top, you can feel the friction of his stubble against your inner thigh and your lips, and the sensation is delicious. You gasp as he brings a thumb up to join his mouth, using it to track a slow circle around your clit while he dips his tongue in and out of you. Then he swaps around, putting first one finger and then another inside you while his tongue does laps of your clit.

You arch your back, leaning your head against the wall behind you, everything still dream-like in the red light. You buck your hips toward his mouth, wanting more, and the pleasure is exquisite as you ride his tongue harder and harder, your fingers clutching at the edge of the countertop, your knuckles white. And then you can't stop yourself from shouting out as you come, too soon for your liking, but there's no stopping it, you writhe against the wall—and then everything goes blinding white. You blink rapidly, confused, wondering whether your orgasm was so powerful it made you go blind.

"Fuck, my photographs!" you hear Jan swear. Your eyes adjust to the light and you realize that the light panel is behind you. You must have knocked the switch on as you were thrashing with pleasure. You suddenly feel very naked in the brightness, and pull the gown closed around you.

Jan has bolted into action, trying to save the prints and the negatives, but it's too late. The ones soaking in the trays have faded completely, as if they got amnesia and forgot what images were printed on them just seconds ago.

He stands over his trays, his face crumpled in disappointment. The only two that survived are the close-up of your breast and the graceful one of your neck and chin. They could be of anyone—the only identifying mark is the freckle on your breast, but only you and a very few others would know that.

You climb off the counter, your knees postorgasm jelly. "I must have pressed the light switch with my back," you say, wrapping your arms around him. "I'm so sorry."

He envelops you, his tongue searching out your mouth again, and the kiss is so passionate, you feel absolved. Then he balances his chin lightly on top of your

a girl walks into a bar

79

head. "I'm just sorry you didn't get to see all the shots we took."

"It's okay, I saw enough," you say. "I'm sorry you didn't get to see your prints, either."

"At least I saw them in real life from behind the camera." He traces a finger down the side of your face and plants a gentle kiss on your forehead. "And then again in extreme close-up just now. I wish I had a photographic memory."

You blush furiously. "Come on, let's get out of here, before these fumes get us completely stoned."

BACK IN THE STUDIO, you sink down on a couch, a little dazed. Jan still has an enormous bulge in his pants, and the idea of another round is tempting. Should you see what he has to offer? Or has the ride been wild enough for one night? Perhaps it's time to get out of here.

❧ If you decide to stay and finish what you started, go to page 81.

❧ If you're ready to leave, go to page 240.

❧ You've decided to stay and finish what you started

JAN DIMS THE STUDIO lights and goes to the kitchen to fetch the rest of the wine. You walk over to the motorbike and run a finger across the smooth chrome tank. You notice that the bike is bolted to the floor, a frame holding it upright so it can't topple over, so you swing a leg over and sit on the saddle. The leather seat feels cool between your legs, where you're still radiating post-orgasmic heat.

Jan appears next to you, puts the wine down on the floor, and turns on the industrial-strength fan that he uses for fashion shoots.

"Here's the wind in your hair, just like the real thing," he says, swiveling the fan so that it's full on you.

The gust blasts your hair back off your face, at the same time blowing your robe away from your body and out behind you like a superhero's cape, revealing your naked body once again. Your skin puckers into goose bumps, and you squeal and grab for the edges of the gown. Jan shifts the fan so that it's blowing past you instead of directly on you. Clutching the long handlebars, you shimmy as far forward on the leather seat as you can, so there's space for him behind you.

"Want a ride?" you offer.

He smiles, considering. Then he swings a leg over the bike behind you.

"So, where are you taking me?" he asks, running his hands around your waist and holding on tight.

"All the way, if you're lucky," you say, and it's corny, but you like it, along with the feel of his arms wrapped around you and his body tight against you. And if you're not mistaken, there's a certain hardness pressing against your back that's very difficult to ignore. You decide it's time to take pity on him. So you climb carefully off the bike, turn around, and mount it again, this time facing him.

He leans into you, kissing you hungrily. Reaching around behind you, he pulls you up against his lap, so that you're straddling him, your feet wrapped behind him on the tail of the bike. The feel of him hard against you gets you excited all over again.

You drop your legs and reach for his crotch, frantically undoing his buckle and then the buttons of his jeans, to discover that he's not wearing any underwear. His cock springs out of his trousers and you run your hand over it. He groans loudly at your touch, growing even harder as you clasp your palm around his cock

Helena L. Paige

and move your hand up and down the length of it, feeling the vein on the side pulsing against your palm like something alive.

"I want you inside me," you whisper, and not having to be invited twice, Jan holds you steady with one hand and reaches into his back pocket for his wallet with the other. He manages to open and fish around in it one-handed, pulling out a condom as you bite at his neck, still stroking his rock-hard erection. He drops the wallet on the floor and tears the packaging open with his teeth. You take the condom from him and use both hands to roll it on to him, smoothing it down the length of his cock.

Unable to wait another second, he eases you backward, then lifts both your stilettoed feet up onto his shoulders so that he has full access to you. Then he runs his thumb up and down your slit. "Now," you urge, and he slips his cock inside you.

He fills every inch of you, and you moan with pleasure. Then his mouth is on your neck and he's sucking, then biting, then sucking again as he rides you, slowly at first, and then gradually picking up speed, until he's pounding into you harder and harder and harder. And you realize that while he's really close to coming, it's going to take you a little longer. But you've already had one earth-shattering orgasm tonight, and you can feel how urgent he is, so you drop your legs down off his shoulders, pull yourself up against his torso, and whisper, "Come inside me now—I want you to," in his ear, grazing it with your teeth. And he can't help shouting

a girl walks into a bar

83

out as he pushes himself over the edge, and you clasp his back and feel his muscles ripple under his shirt as he shudders out a powerful orgasm.

With him still inside you, you lie back on the tank of the motorbike, a cat-that-ate-the-canary grin on your face. He leans forward, dropping his head sideways onto your naked chest, panting.

LATER, AS THE TAXI pulls away from the studio and Jan waves from the door, you think that maybe losing the prints wasn't such a bad thing after all. You got to have nude photographs taken by a sexy professional photographer who's shot some major superstars, but you'll never have to worry about them popping up on the Internet when you least expect it. You got really lucky tonight, in more ways than one. Now it's time for the comfort of your own home, with a DVD and some popcorn. Or maybe you should drop in on Melissa—you can't wait to tell her about the night you've had.

❧ If you go straight home, go to page 217.

❧ If you swing past Melissa's house on your way home to tell her about your wild night, go to page 249.

Helena S. Paige

84

❧ You've decided to stay at the gallery or go back
   to it

◐ MOST OF THE CROWD has left the exhibition, and you stand alone off to the side of the gallery, clutching an almost-empty glass of indifferent sparkling wine, examining one of the portraits. They don't seem quite so risqué now that you've had a chance to get used to them. You're a little shocked at how fast you've become blasé about looking at another woman's private parts.

Mac reappears beside you, and your stomach flutters.

"Hello again. Have you been enjoying yourself?" She slides those remarkable eyes sideways at you. "You and Jan seemed to be getting along famously, the last I looked."

"Um, yes, I think he went off to his studio." It's impossible to explain what happened with Jan—you're having a little difficulty believing it yourself.

You tilt your glass, then realize there's nothing left in it.

Mac looks at you unblinkingly, then one corner of her mouth lifts. "Would you like some decent champagne, not the faux bubbles they're serving here? I have a bottle of something very delicious chilling upstairs. I've been saving it for just this kind of thirst."

Your mouth is dry, and the thought of icy champagne is very appealing. The idea of hanging out with Mac is appealing, too, even though you find her a little intimidating. Perhaps you should play it safe and head back to the bar. You could always drink more champagne with that cute bartender instead. Or maybe it's time to call it a night.

❧ If you decide to follow Mac, go to page 87.

❧ If you'd rather go back to the bar to flirt with the cute bartender, go to page 186.

❧ If you decide to head straight home, go to page 217.

❧ You've decided to follow Mac

Mac inserts a key into a massive wooden door, and you follow her into a warm, perfumed, shadowy space. She glides forward, flicking switches, and lamps glow to life, revealing the most exotic apartment you've ever seen. Almost every inch of the lime-green walls is covered with photographs, prints, icons, and posters. A Black Madonna stands in an alcove, a string of Mardi Gras beads around her neck and a bunch of fresh poppies standing in a glass next to her. You spot the familiar poster of Che Guevara on the wall—but someone has outlined his mouth in fire-engine-red lipstick and pasted false lashes around his eyes.

There's a tiny kitchen alcove, with a basket of seashells on the counter, and a studio room, with a huge bed piled with colorful cushions in one corner and a draftsman's table under the window. Mac's feet tap across the hardwood floor between pools of rugs, some fluffy and pale, some rich and red. There's something strange about the sound of her shoes on the floor, and you comment on it.

"Ah, I'm wearing my flamenco shoes. And it's only the gallery downstairs, so I can practice my *sevillanas* as much as I please."

You feel more and more like Alice falling down the rabbit hole. What is she talking about?

"I promised you champagne, didn't I?" She twirls to the refrigerator and hauls out a bottle. You're not an expert, but you can see it's the good stuff. Her strong hands make swift work of the cork, easing it out with a delicate pop. The straw-colored liquid foams into tall glasses.

"Your health." She arches an eyebrow as you clink glasses. Why does everything this woman says sound like it means something suggestive?

The champagne is cool and grassy, and you relax a little. Mac goes over to a laptop on the artist's table and presses a few keys. The next minute, the sound of a guitar ripples through the room. It's soothing—until a man's raw voice bursts into song, and invisible hands start clapping.

"It's *cante flamenco*—flamenco singing," says Mac. "It's an integral part of flamenco tradition, along with the dancer and the guitarist. Historically, it's always been about passion. But why don't you sit, and I'll show you?"

"Show me what?"

Her feet clatter out a swift tattoo on the floor, a blur of precise steps.

You blink. "You're going to dance? Now?"

"Why not? Tonight feels like a good night for dancing. Please, make yourself comfortable."

You look around, but apart from the office chair at the table, there's nowhere to sit. You retreat to the bed and perch on the edge. You're not exactly into spontaneous outbreaks of song and dance—that's what musicals are for—but what's the worst that can happen?

Mac moves to the center of the room and kicks aside a few rugs. Slowly, teasingly, she removes her jewelry, placing her chains, pendants, and bracelets on the kitchen counter, although the earrings stay.

Then her body tenses, seems to grow taller. Slowly her arms rise, curving sinuously above her head, her wrists and fingers describing smaller circles of their own. Her back arches, her breasts rise and heave. Then she explodes, her heels cracking down on to the floor, starting to hammer out the same rhythm as the frantically strumming guitars, her feet moving so fast it's impossible to see the individual steps.

You sit as if turned to stone. Time slows. You've never seen anything so sensual in your life. Mac turns and turns, her arms braced, her feet beating out a complex rhythm, her rounded bottom shuddering with every step. She seizes her skirt and swishes it from side to side. Sweat pearls on her bare collarbone and starts to trickle down between her breasts. It's clear from the way

a girl walks into a bar

they move and jounce under the clinging lace fabric of her top that she is braless.

At last the music slows down, and so do Mac's feet. Then she bows so low, it's a wonder her breasts don't spill out. It isn't until she clatters to the kitchen to gulp a glass of water that the spell is broken, and you start applauding.

She gathers up the bottle of champagne and flops on to the bed next to you, her chest still heaving.

"That was amazing! I'm so impressed."

"It's not only an ancient art form, it's the most amazing exercise," she says. "But it makes me so hot!"

Before you can think about what exactly that means, she seizes the hem of her top and peels it off over her head. Her breasts bounce into view, heavier and bigger than you expected, but firm and taut. The chocolate-rose nipples stand out hard against softer areolas.

You're out of your depth, but while you're racking your brain for the appropriate comment ("Um, did you notice you'd taken your top off?"), Mac turns to you, that direct look again.

"Would you like to touch them?"

You're tempted, but this is all a bit overwhelming. The wild music, the dancing, another woman's bare breasts—and now she wants you to touch them. You're intrigued and a little turned on, but you're nervous, too. Part of you is eager to stay and see what happens—when will you ever get a chance like this again?—but perhaps you'd better make an excuse and duck out before you

Helena S. Paige

get in too deep. You could head back to the bar for a nightcap—at least that's familiar territory.

❧ If you decide to stick around and see what happens, go to page 92.

❧ If this is all too much for you, and you decide to head back to the safety of the bar, go to page 186.

a girl walks into a bar

❧ You've decided to stick around and see what
happens

 "So, WOULD YOU LIKE to touch them?" she asks
again.

Wow, that *is* direct. You're floored. "I . . . um, I'm not
a—I've never . . . I'm not that way inclined . . ."

"I didn't ask if you were a lesbian. I asked if you
wanted to touch." She grins, raises her strong, curving
arms, and links her hands behind her head. "I promise I
won't bite. Well, not just yet."

You have to admit that you're fascinated. And her
boobs are absolutely luscious.

"Here." Mac reaches for one of your hands, tugs it
gently. She doesn't put it on her breast, she places it on
her rib cage just below. You can't help it: your hand slides
upward, cups, and the weight of her breast falls into
your hand as easily as a ripe fruit. It's much softer than it

looks, and the skin is finely textured. You squeeze softly, and are rewarded with the feel of her nipple growing diamond-hard against your palm.

She makes a little noise of satisfaction. "The other one is getting jealous, you know."

You reach out with both hands now, running your fingers over her heated flesh, exploring the silky curves. Tentatively, then more boldly, you finger the nipples, intrigued at the way they respond to your touch.

"Very good," purrs Mac, sinking back on to the mass of pillows. "Now perhaps with your mouth?"

This feels weird, but you don't want to stop. You lean forward over her torso, then pause. "I don't know how . . ."

"So let me show you. Relax . . ." She sits up, and you catch the scent of her skin. Deft fingers slide the straps of your dress down. As neatly as unpeeling a banana, she bares you to the waist, rolling down the fabric of your dress and your bra with it. You shiver from nerves and the air on your exposed skin, but before you have time to think, Mac leans in and closes her mouth around one of your nipples. Oh god. The double shock—*There's a woman sucking my breast*, along with the sudden flare of pleasure—leaves you speechless. Her mouth is warm and wet, and her tongue is sliding and flicking, and you don't care who's doing it, because it feels great.

You barely notice Mac gently pressing you back onto the pillows, or leaning over you. All you can think about is the mouth traveling over first one breast, then the other, followed by her strong fingers, rolling, tweaking, stroking. Time stretches, and as if from far away, you hear yourself making faint whimpering sounds.

Without warning, Mac sits up.

"What's wrong?" You don't want her to stop.

"*Chica*, we're wearing way too many clothes. You may have noticed downstairs: I'm more comfortable naked than I am dressed."

Whoa. Does this mean what you think—are you ready for this? But Mac has already stripped off her skirt. You're somehow not surprised by the fact that she's not wearing underwear, or by the red jewel winking in her navel, but what does come as a shock is her smooth mound, which is completely bare. She stands by the bed dressed only in earrings and her black flamenco heels.

You stare at her, unable to tear your eyes away from her naked pussy. "I—but in the photos, I mean, you're not . . ." you stammer.

"I like to change things up a bit. Sometimes I go wild. Sometimes I go bare. And it's better this way for tonight. It means you get to see e-ve-ry-thing." Mac's eyes narrow as she drawls out the last word.

Before you can process this, she says, "I think we need to get that dress off, don't you?" You sit up, moving to accommodate her as she takes the hem and tugs it over your head. She makes short work of your bra, now somewhere around your waist, and then presses you back down again. Her eyes glitter in the lamplight as

Helena S. Paige

she looks down at you, now only in your purple G-string and heels.

"Aha," she purrs. "I knew there was a tiger under that tidy exterior." Then she hooks a finger into the elastic of your G-string and starts to slide it down.

Oh god. This is it, the point of no return. You're in bed with a naked woman who is removing the last of your clothes.

One thing's for sure, a certain part of your anatomy is keen. As Mac draws the lace down past your thighs, you can feel that you're hugely aroused, and she knows it—your panties are soaked through, and she chuckles. "I think you're going to taste very sweet, *chica*."

You feel an unmistakable gush at her words, and let yourself go limp as she nudges a smooth, warm thigh between your legs. But she doesn't touch any part of you; instead she leans over you, on all fours, and commands: "Shut your eyes."

You obey, and the next second her warm mouth comes down on yours. *Omigod, omigod I'm kissing another woman,* goes through your head for one nanosecond before you realize how soft her mouth feels compared with the guys you've kissed. She tastes of cinnamon and the grassy edge of the champagne. Her lips nudge at yours, her tongue flickers as she slides it into your mouth. She takes no prisoners: she tugs and sucks and slants her mouth against yours, opening you up to her, her fingers cradling your head.

Your head is spinning when she breaks for air, still

a girl walks into a bar

poised over you. You reach for her face, and gently lick that beauty spot that's been intriguing you all evening. You feel the muscles of her face move as she smiles, but then she's sliding away from you.

"If you've never had sex with another woman before, there's one thing you need to know. No one knows how to go down on you like another woman. Shall I prove it to you?"

You can't speak. You can only stare in fascination as she starts snaking her tongue down your torso. Her hair trails against your skin, rousing little flares as it goes. You see the goose bumps rising, your nipples leaping to attention as she slides down and down.

You're suddenly embarrassed. You have no sexy piercings or daring tattoos, and your bush only gets a conservative bikini wax now and again—you've never had the courage to try anything more dramatic. Her tongue passes your navel, and you panic. But before you can get any words out, you feel her hands pressing your thighs apart and then the incredible rush of her breath on your pussy.

You tense, hungry, nervous, and ferociously curious, trying to anticipate what happens next. Then you yelp and convulse helplessly: she has homed in on your clit with absolute accuracy and is sucking it—first gently and then hard. Her soft, wet lips pull at it rhythmically as you thrash around, trying to adjust to the intensity of the sensations.

"Oh god, it's too much!" you gasp, and the mad-

dening sucking slows. Next you feel her hot tongue—it feels huge—parting your labia. Her fingers spread your lips wide, and then wipe the slick wetness, her saliva and your juice, onto your thighs.

Your whole world is concentrated on her tongue, which is tasting you, licking the opening of your pussy and your lips very slowly. Then it presses inside, sliding up into you. The feeling is overwhelming, and you gasp again. Slowly Mac's tongue withdraws and slides up and out to flick at your clit again, but this time, her knotted fingers push into you. She's not gentle—the contrast between the soft, skilled dance of her tongue on your clit and the powerful thrusts of her fingers has you moaning and writhing, feeling the muscles clench, the onset of orgasm.

Then you're bereft. Mac has pulled away, leaving you bucking with your hips, flailing for her with your hands. "Don't stop, I can't—you must—"

She lies on top of you, pinning you with her warm, strong body, the unfamiliar sensation of breasts against your own, her skin soft and smooth.

"*Chica*, if I let you come now, you might want to run away too soon. And I have lots of things I want to do to and for you tonight."

She rolls over next to you. "Wouldn't you like to get up close and personal with my cunt?"

She uses the word matter-of-factly, and it's *hot*.

"I dunno—I . . ."

"Oh come on. I saw you staring in the gallery. Have

a girl walks into a bar

you ever had a chance to really look at another woman this way?"

She's right: you're curious about those deep rose and chocolate-lilac folds you saw in the gallery. She reads your silence correctly, lies back on the pillows, and spreads her legs with the ease of a dancer. You clamber between them, panting, still feeling the dense buildup of sexual pressure in your lower belly and pelvis.

"What do I do? I mean, what do you want me to . . . Should I . . . ?"

"Just look. And then if you want, you can touch. And if you like that, you can taste."

You lower yourself between her legs and take a good, hard look. It's like the gallery again, except this time you can almost taste her scent. Her bare mound is cocoa-pink. You reach out a hesitant finger, and find that the flesh is resistant, soft, springy.

You trail your fingers a little lower. Mac's labia are swollen and the slightly frilled edges are moist. You touch tentatively, then slide a finger between her lips, spreading them apart. They're gleaming wet, shining in the soft light like the inside of a pink conch shell. And you can see the pearl of her clit under its hood of skin— it's deep red and throbbing slightly. Very carefully, cautiously, you lap at it.

It feels surprisingly hard under your tongue, a little marble of flesh, and you lick again. Mac groans, which gives you a bit more confidence.

Um, what should you do next? You lick more boldly,

sweeping your tongue up and down between her labia. The taste is pretty damn sexy, and so is the juice all over your mouth. Your face is an inch from her vagina, and you're curious about that, too. You prod gently at the dark opening between her fleshy lips with your fingertips, then knot two fingers together and push them into her. There's a momentary resistance and you hesitate—what if you hurt her?—and then your fingers are being enveloped by her clasping pussy. Mac is sighing and curving her hips up rhythmically, so you have to be doing something right. You try to match her rhythm, and she starts giving short, cut-off cries like you were earlier. Your own unresolved need tugs in your pussy.

Then she reaches down and clamps a hand around your wrist, stopping the movement of your hand.

"Sorry, am I doing it wrong?"

"No, you're doing great. But I want you up here with me when I come."

You scramble alongside her, and she lies half-facing you, one leg draped over yours. She captures one of your hands and places it over her breast. Then she reaches between her legs and starts circling her index finger on her clit. You're disappointed for a minute—until her other hand slides between your legs, and you feel her nimble fingers echoing her own movements. She builds a rhythm on your clit, then slides two fingers inside you. You're practically a wetland down there—they're going to slap a conservation order on you any minute.

"You too. Try for yourself."

a girl walks into a bar

You get the message and reach for her pussy. Mimicking her movements—which is hard because the feeling of her fingers plunging in and out of you, then rubbing your clit, hitting the good spot, are overwhelming—you alternate between finger-fucking her and massaging her clit.

You're so close to coming, but she senses it, and pulls her hand away or softens the pressure every time. Then her pupils dilate. Is this it? Her eyes clamp shut, her head rolls back on the pillow, and she screams. You can feel her vagina clenching and unclenching on your fingers, incredibly fast, almost fluttering, spurting hot juice down into your palm. Her spine arches so hard, her back leaves the bed, followed by spasm after spasm.

Then the room is quiet except for her panting. You're feeling conflicting emotions—you're proud of yourself for giving Mac such an intense orgasm, you're boiling with desire, and you're a bit anxious: What about you?

"Don't worry, *chica*, it's your turn now." It's as if she heard your thoughts.

She rears up over you, hair and eyes wild. She pushes your knees up and apart, then crouches over your cunt. Her fingers slide back inside you, picking up the rhythm again. You're so close, you can feel the storm building inside, your hips coming off the bed—and at that moment she swoops down and fastens her mouth over your pussy, her strong tongue licking your lips, swirling on your clit.

It tips you over the edge, the intensity rushing

through you like champagne bubbling in your veins, the exploding tension, the glorious spasms of pleasure—you almost black out. Dimly you're aware that you're bucking like a mustang and screaming your head off.

Slowly, the room stops spinning. The rushing noise you can hear in your ears is your own blood pounding. Your limbs feel heavy. Your pussy is awash—you can feel the stickiness of your juices all over your thighs.

Mac gets to her feet—she's still wearing those black heels—and you feel a little lost, but she's pouring more champagne. She comes back to the bed and curls up next to you like a big cat, clinks her glass against yours.

"Congratulations. Your first time with a woman. And you came with flying colors!"

You giggle. You're too satisfied by the slow throb in your lower body to worry about the strangeness of the situation—hell, Che Guevara in drag just watched a woman go down on you!

Minutes pass as your breathing goes back to normal. Eventually Mac sit ups, takes your face in her hands, and smacks a kiss first on your mouth, then your forehead.

"That was fantastic," she says. "You know where I live now, so don't be a stranger. Maybe next time—if there is a next time—you might even meet my girlfriend."

"What?" You're stunned. "Your girlfriend? But I thought . . ."

"Oh, come on now. Did you think I was going to make an honest woman of you?"

a girl walks into a bar

You feel foolish. "No . . ."

Mac strokes your hair, an oddly maternal gesture. "Don't be silly, *chica*. That was great, but you're not a lesbian, are you?" She leans back and runs her eyes over you. "Although you've certainly got potential."

"But why—I mean, if you have someone?"

"Daniella lives in another city—she's a partner in a good law firm. And my dance company is based here. We both love our work, so we do the whole long-distance thing. It's been five years. Sometimes it's tough, but it's not all bad. There are certain advantages . . . like tonight."

"Will you tell her?"

"Of course. Every. Little. Detail. She'll be so turned on."

You blush scarlet. Oh god, you've been such a fool. You've been a conquest so that a couple can share titillating tales. You hang your head as you start to reach under the bed for your scattered clothes.

Mac tugs at your shoulder. "I can see what you're thinking. But you went out tonight with your big-girl panties on, didn't you?" She holds up the purple G-string, twirling it round her finger. "I could see you were straight. But I could also see there was a very hungry little pussycat in there. And you're gorgeous, all that luscious skin, that wide-eyed look. How could I resist?"

You give a little sniff, but she's right. You may have fucked a woman and loved it, but it's not like you plan on changing your entire life, coming out to all your family and friends, shacking up with her, wrangling over family holidays together. Tonight was a walk on the wild side, and boy, was it wild.

You pull yourself together, and give Mac a watery smile. Then you find your dress and step into it, not bothering with your bra, which you stuff into your handbag. You hold out your hand for your G-string, and she drops a kiss on it before pressing it into your palm.

"I'll walk you to the door," she says, leaping to her feet, still stark naked except for those heels. As you follow her across the room, watching her long violin-shaped back, undulating bottom and shapely legs, you feel a leap of remembered desire in your tender pussy. In the tiny hallway, she presses herself against you, slides her tongue into your mouth again. It doesn't feel weird, it feels great, and you kiss her back with real enthusiasm and gratitude.

Her eyes glint. "Off you go, before we start all over again. Hmm, maybe we could arrange a threesome next time Danni's in town . . . ?"

That brings you back to your senses. "OK, um thanks." *What's the etiquette for situations like these? "Thank you for being the first woman to lick my pussy"? "Thanks for the great girl-on-girl orgasm"?*

"Um, that was great. Better than great. But . . . don't take this the wrong way, I don't think I'll be back."

She laughs. "Whatever you say, *chica*." And then you're wobbling down the stairs on loose legs, your

pussy still throbbing faintly. As you reach the street, you realize: Mac never even asked you your name.

The idea of your familiar sofa, with a DVD and popcorn, suddenly seems very appealing. Or you could go past your local neighborhood coffee shop and pick up a hot chocolate on the way home.

❧ To go straight home, go to page 217.

❧ If you're not ready to go home yet, go to page 240.

❧ To go home via your neighborhood coffee shop, go to page 242.

Helena L. Paige

🐍 You've decided to share a taxi with the sexy older guy

 You crumple the "Immaculata" flyer and drop it back into your handbag. On another night, you might consider going to check out the exhibition, but not with a man this compelling offering to share his taxi with you. There's something about him that makes your knees go a little bendy. It has something to do with the way he commands whatever space he's in. He doesn't just pay rent, he owns it.

"I don't see any reason why we can't share a taxi," he says. "Think of the environment—carbon footprint and all that."

"I suppose it would be the responsible thing to do," you concede.

He laughs and holds the door open for you as you climb in. As he goes around to the other side of the taxi, you look out of the window and see the huge bodyguard wave at you, then fold himself into that incredible sports car before revving the engine and roaring off into the night. You wonder how things might have turned out if you'd decided to go with him instead, but before you can dwell on it, Miles climbs into the taxi and settles in next to you, filling the space with the scent of cedar and leather.

The driver leans over from the front seat and waits for his instructions.

"So, where to?" Miles asks.

"I was just going to head home," you say. "I was supposed to meet my friend here for a drink earlier, but she let me down at the last minute. She had to work late. Her boss can be a bit of a controlling bastard."

Miles raises an eyebrow. "Speaking of working late, you're not hungry by any chance? I've been so busy closing a deal, I haven't eaten since lunch, and doing business always makes me ravenous."

"I am a bit hungry. What did you have in mind?" you ask.

"I know this great sushi place not far from here; their sashimi is world-class. And their sake is excellent, too. I was just going to head there for a late dinner. Would you like to join me?"

You consider him, trying to decide what to do. Maybe you should just call it a night and go home. Maybe the taxi could drop you off at your local coffee shop for your favorite hot-chocolate fix. But good sushi is hard to find—and this man is seriously attractive.

The driver clears his throat, and you notice that the

meter has been running the whole time. You need to make a decision, and quickly.

🍃 If you decide to go for sushi with the charming older guy, go to page 108.

🍃 If you ask the taxi driver to take you straight home, go to page 217.

🍃 If the taxi drops you off at your local late-night coffee shop, go to page 242.

a girl walks into a bar

 You've decided to go for sushi

"THAT SOUNDS GOOD. I like sushi."

The taxi driver gives an audible sigh of relief.

"Excellent," says Miles, then gives the driver an address and quick directions on how to get there.

After a short drive, the taxi turns onto a quiet street. You look out of the window, but you don't see any visible restaurants or shops. Miles pays the driver, then gets out and opens your door for you. You try not to flash your negligible panties as you slide out of the taxi. It's not as easy as the Hollywood actresses make it look.

You cross the pavement and Miles leads you to a recessed door. It doesn't look anything like a restaurant from the outside: there are no signs or names on any of the windows, which are curtained so you can't see inside. So you're amazed when you step through the door and find yourself in an intimate and discreetly decorated

Japanese restaurant. The staff and most of the diners appear to be Japanese, which is always a good sign.

An elegant woman in a kimono bustles up to you, a welcoming smile on her face. "Mr. Cornuti, so glad to see you again! Table for two?"

"Cornuti!" you blurt out as light dawns and your stomach plummets. "Oh my god, you're Miles Cornuti!"

It's hardly a common name—you didn't put two and two together earlier because the taxi driver mangled it.

He nods in acknowledgment before greeting the hostess. "Hello, Katsuko, it's good to see you, too. May we have two seats at the counter, please?"

She guides you toward the back of the restaurant to a counter that looks directly into a modern kitchen, where two Japanese chefs are working side by side, masterfully slicing fish and rolling out rice. You take your seats beside each other, facing the prep area, which is designed so that diners can watch the chefs preparing the sushi. It's an art, and quite something to see. You've heard that they spend decades in Japan just learning to prepare the rice before they're ever allowed anywhere near a piece of fish.

The chefs nod politely at you, then get back to their sharp knives and rolling mats, chatting to each other quietly in Japanese. The taller one, wielding a knife that looks more like a sword, effortlessly does a Zorro on a giant slab of tuna, transforming it into perfect sashimi, the muscles in his forearms rippling as he works. These guys are clearly the real deal.

The restaurant is half full, and there's nobody else

a girl walks into a bar

up at the counter. You're sitting so close to Miles that his arm and leg brush against yours, causing a ripple of excitement through your body.

Once your companion has exchanged pleasantries with the hostess and ordered some sake, she disappears, leaving you alone with menus. You seize the opportunity to grill him: "I can't believe it. You're Miles Cornuti, the famous media mogul!"

"Hardly famous," he says.

"Of course you are—you own dozens of magazines and a newspaper, and then there are all the imprints and the e-publishing ventures."

Katsuko reappears with a carafe of sake. Miles pours some into two delicate handleless cups and offers you one. "Try this, it's really good. Apparently they fly it in from Japan every month."

"Don't try to change the subject," you say, cradling the cup in both hands and taking a few sips, enjoying the silky liquid easing its way down. "I've heard lots about you. I have a friend who's a writer for one of your publications."

"I hope it's not the same friend who stood you up tonight? The one whose boss is a real—what did you call him again?"

"Umm . . ." Now it's your turn to squirm.

"I do believe you said he was some sort of bastard?"

"Controlling bastard," you squeak, heat radiating off your face.

"Ah yes, that's right. Controlling bastard at your service, ma'am."

You fidget in your seat, grateful to be sitting side by side, so you don't have to deal with his teasing stare.

"Actually, I think what she meant was . . ." you scramble, trying to backtrack.

"Go on," he says, smirking. "I want to see how you get yourself out of this one."

"More sake?" you say, reaching for the carafe and pretending to refill both your cups.

Miles cracks a grin. "Here's to controlling-bastard bosses everywhere," he says, holding up his cup. You click your cup against his and take another few sips, praying for a quick change of subject. Melissa is going to kill you. How are you going to explain that you went out to dinner with her boss and let slip what she said about him?

You do a mental stock-take of everything else she's ever told you about him, coming up with superrich, powerful, and yes, very demanding to work for. But that makes sense. You don't get to be a media mogul by being a pushover. You get to be a media mogul by being a controlling bastard. But—and more important—why hasn't she ever mentioned how incredibly hot he is?

You study him surreptitiously while pretending to read the menu. Tall, good body, charismatic, confident. And he has that George Clooney crinkly-smiling-eye look, and it works for him. But still, what are you doing? *This is your best friend's boss.* You shouldn't be checking him out, you should be getting out of there faster than a sumo wrestler at a Weight Watchers meeting. But it wouldn't hurt to stay for just a quick tuna and avocado hand-roll, surely?

a girl walks into a bar

When you eventually look at the menu, you realize the whole thing is in Japanese. You turn it over to see if there are English translations, or at least pictures of the dishes on the reverse, but no such luck.

"So, you say this place is the real deal? What do you recommend?" you ask nonchalantly, as if you read Japanese every day of the week, hoping you aren't holding the menu upside down.

He leans over and you're expecting him to say something knowing or pretentious, or to offer to order for you, but instead he says, "I haven't got a clue. I always ask Katsuko to recommend something. The first time I came here I tried to be clever, and I accidentally ordered one of their more . . . unusual delicacies."

"What happened?"

He pulls a face. "It turned out I had asked for cod sperm."

You almost spit your sake across the counter.

"The chefs and waitresses thought it was hilarious. They only told me what I was eating after I'd swallowed the first bite. I made their night." He nods at one of the chefs, who salutes back with a flourish of his knife.

"What did it taste like?"

"Actually, it was a bit like squid. But no more fish semen for me. These days I stick to safer dishes."

You can't resist the temptation to flirt. "So you're saying you like to play it safe?"

He gazes at you intently. "That depends on who I'm playing with."

A flicker of sexual tension darts between you.

"And what about you?" he asks. "Would you consider yourself the adventurous type?"

"I like to think I'm always up for a bit of adventure," you say.

"Well, let's see if that's true." He raises his hand, and within seconds Katsuko is back at your side.

"I'll have my usual, please: the tuna sashimi, some salmon *maki*, and some wasabi parcels—and then my friend and I were thinking we might try something a little bit different for a change. What do you recommend?"

You're sure there's a mischievous glint in Katsuko's eye. "Tonight we have fresh *unagi*, Mr. Cornuti."

She points at a tank against the wall of the restaurant. An assortment of rather odd-looking creatures are inside, including some very spiny sea urchins, a few starfish latched to the sides of the tank, and half a dozen eels slithering around, tying themselves in knots. "As you can see, we also have fresh *uni*. And we have our usual more traditional delicacies," she says.

"*Uni?*" you ask, your voice a nervous rasp.

"Sea urchin. The reproductive organs," Katsuko informs you, her face impassive.

Miles looks at you. "I'm game—if you are."

"I'll have what he's having," you say, trying not to blanch.

"Let's try the *uni*. And bring us one of those traditional delicacies, too, please," says Miles.

While Katsuko turns to instruct the chefs in quick Japanese, you sit back and take another sip of sake, wondering what on earth you've gotten yourself into.

Once your order's in, you find the conversation flows easily. He's more forthcoming about his personal life than you would have expected from someone of his standing, and your guilt about Melissa starts to fade; it feels not so much like having dinner with your friend's boss as hanging out with a friend. A smoking-hot friend, but a friend nonetheless.

You discover he's been divorced for a couple of years now, but he gets on well with his ex and his two step-children, both of whom are almost grown by now. He mentions that he's a workaholic, which is what led to the divorce. He's always been married to his business—that's fairly well-known—but you can't help admiring his commitment to his work. It's part of what makes him so compelling. And while you can detect the controlling aspect of his personality lurking around the edges, the bastard part seems to be mercifully absent so far.

"So now I've told you all about my love life. What about yours?" he asks.

You look down. You don't think babbling about the stony desert that is your current romantic life is going to be very appealing, so you decide to keep it simple. "Nope, there's no one right now."

"No boyfriend?"

You shake your head.

He grins. "Girlfriend?"

Helena L. Paige

"Are you hoping I'll say yes? Isn't that what all guys fantasize about?"

"Not this guy," he says, draining his cup.

Katsuko interrupts once again, but you forgive her as she places several little plates of food on the counter. You cast your eye over the offerings, relieved to discover that there's nothing you don't recognize, and it all looks delicious. As you're about to dig in, you notice that one of the chefs is over at the tank, fishing something out of it, and you realize you're not quite out of the woods yet.

Miles twirls his chopsticks, which of course he handles like a pro, and you pick up yours, hoping you won't drop food down your cleavage or stab yourself in the eye. But at the first bite of the succulent little parcel you've snagged, you forget to worry about your chopstick technique. You hadn't realized how hungry you were—or perhaps it's because the food is so good. The fish is so fresh it melts in your mouth, and there seems to be the perfect amount of every ingredient in each bite.

Some of the pieces are too big to navigate into your mouth whole, and you're relieved when Miles abandons his chopsticks and simply picks up one of the rolls with his fingers. Oh, thank heavens, he's human, you think, following suit.

At one point while you're discussing the rise of e-books, Miles pauses mid-sentence, then reaches his hand up to your face. "May I?" he asks.

You hold your breath, unsure what he's to do. Surely he's not going to kiss you? He leans in close, then brushes a stray grain of rice from your cheek. But he

a girl walks into a bar

115

doesn't just dab at it quickly with one finger. Instead he holds your chin in his palm and brushes his thumb across the width of your cheek. The intimacy of his touch is shocking, the pad of his thumb soft on your skin, and your body instantly wants more. Once his fingers are gone, you swipe at your scorching cheek, feeling for other imaginary grains of rice, a little embarrassed at both your inept sushi-eating and how you reacted to his touch.

And then Katsuko appears once more and begins to stack up the empty plates while Miles pours out the last of the sake into your cups. Once the counter is cleared, she returns and places two little plates down between you.

"*Uni*," she says, nodding at the one plate.

The plate contains something that looks a bit like sushi rolls, with rice luxuriously wrapped in dark seaweed. But lodged on top of the rice are thick wedges of bright orange flesh. It's textured like a tongue, and it looks almost spongy. The second plate holds even worse horrors—what appear to be two giant eyeballs. Each one is slightly bigger than a gumball, and they still have bits of flesh and fiber attached around the edges. Your stomach churns at the sight of them, and they stare back up at you, equally unimpressed.

You pick up a chopstick and prod at one of the orange fleshy things, and you're sure it quivers as you touch it. You snatch your hand back. Surely the monstrous thing isn't still alive?

Miles laughs. "Aren't you the girl who told me she was up for a bit of adventure?"

Helena L. Paige

"Aren't you the guy who told me that he accidentally ate cod semen?" you shoot back. "So this should be a walk in the park for you . . . What did you say this was again?"

The more handsome of the two chefs, who is watching the show with frank interest, bows in the direction of the spongy orange tongue thing: "*Uni*—sea urchin."

"And *that*?" you ask, tentatively pointing at an eyeball with your chopstick.

"Tuna eyeball. Big delicacy in Japan," the chef says, unable to hide his grin.

"Fantastic," you say, trying to sound convincing.

Miles reaches forward with his chopsticks, going straight for an eyeball. He grasps it and then raises it, not taking his eyes off you for a second. "Here's to adventure," he says.

You poke at the remaining eyeball, then pick it up, trying to keep your hand steady. It's so fat and slippery, you have to take care it doesn't pop out of your chopsticks and bounce along the counter. It looks disgusting, and as you get it closer to your mouth you realize that it doesn't smell so good, either. But you stay firm and lock eyes with Miles, who has a challenging expression on his face.

Both of you maneuver the eyeballs closer and closer to your mouths, watching each other carefully.

You stare in horror as Miles opens his mouth, and it hits you: if he puts that thing in his mouth, you'll never be able to kiss him. And you realize that's all you've been thinking about doing since you met him. So while

there's no way you can put an eyeball in your mouth, more important, he can't, either.

With a shudder, you drop your eyeball. "I can't, I give up. You win!" you yelp.

"You give up?"

"Yes, you win. That's just too disgusting for words!"

"Oh, thank god!" he says, dropping his eyeball onto the plate, where it skids around before coming to a flabby stop next to its mate, both pupils staring up at you dolefully.

"I concede—when it comes to food, you're more daring than I am!"

He smirks, but then stops and leans toward you. "Wait—what do you mean when it comes to food?"

By now you're only inches apart. You feel the fizz of sexual energy that's been building between you all night. The urge to just lean forward and kiss him is overwhelming.

Katsuko glides up to the table again, and clears away the untouched *uni* and the eyeballs.

"How about dessert?" Miles asks.

"What did you have in mind?"

"Well, they have green-tea ice cream . . ."

Your narrow escape from death by eyeball has made you bold. "How about something a little more decadent?" you say, throwing caution to the wind and sliding your leg between his.

"I think you're right," he says slowly. "I'm not in the mood for ice cream, either. Shall we go back to my place? I'm sure we can find the perfect dessert there."

You hesitate for a minute, wrestling with your conscience, but he's too magnetic for you to walk away at this point. Sorry, Melissa.

Miles gestures for the bill, then takes your hand as you head to the cash register.

"Thank you for dinner," you say as you stand together waiting for the credit-card machine to spit out its slip.

The corners of his piercing eyes crinkle, and then he leans into you, brushing his mouth against your ear as he whispers, "I wasn't going to eat that eyeball at any point tonight."

You stand on tiptoes to reach his ear and whisper back: "And I wasn't going to let you."

OUTSIDE ON THE PAVEMENT, waiting for your taxi to arrive, Miles finally leans down, cups your chin, and kisses you deeply. His mouth is hot and hungry. Your knees feel like they might give way, and he must sense this, because he puts both arms around you and holds you firmly against him as you kiss.

When you're both breathless, he pulls back. "Before we go, I need to tell you—I wasn't joking about being adventurous." He laces the fingers of his hands in yours. "Are you sure you're up for it?"

"I'm not sure I understand."

"I just like to do things slightly differently."

You have no doubt about that—you imagine this man does everything slightly differently.

a girl walks into a bar

"But I can guarantee you'll enjoy it," he says when you don't respond.

"How do you know?"

"I was right about the sushi, wasn't I?"

Your mind whirls through the possibilities. You weren't lying about liking a bit of adventure. Bungee jumping isn't entirely out of the question, and you've been known to read the odd saucy book—but you have no intention of getting tied up in a love dungeon. But he's so suave, you think, he couldn't possibly be into anything too crazy. And he *was* right about the sushi. You waver, trying to decide what to do.

Sometimes it's best to leave things on a high note. After all, you've had your fun with Miles Cornuti. Maybe it's time to call it a night, having lost nothing more than an eyeball challenge and perhaps a sliver of dignity. He is Melissa's boss, after all. No man—however hot—is worth risking a friendship over. And you could always swing by your local late-night coffee shop—maybe all you need for dessert is hot chocolate. But those George Clooney eyes . . .

❧ If you decide to go back to Miles's place, go to page 121.

❧ If you decide not to go home with Miles, go to page 144.

❧ If you go past your local late-night coffee shop on your way home, go to page 242.

Helena S. Paige

❧ You've decided to go back to Miles's place

Wow. You STAND IN the double-volume entrance hall, attempting to take in what you're seeing. Miles's house is a masterpiece of understated luxury—it looks like it's about to be photographed for *Minimalist Design Weekly*. The white walls showcase an eclectic mix of art. There are beautiful classic pieces mixed in with the kind of modern art you've always suspected a two-year-old could do, even though you're sure each one of these is worth the GDP of a small country. There's not a thing out of place, and certainly no stray coffee mugs littered about. The subtle lighting softens the white stone surfaces—even the downlighters have downlighters.

He takes you on a guided tour through the open-plan living room, dining room, and kitchen, and then up stairs that float effortlessly and seemingly unsupported out of the wall. The ceilings are so high you could play volleyball inside.

There's no question about your destination, and your excitement builds as he leads you toward the bedroom. Are you really going to do this? Sleep with your best friend's boss? You still feel a slight twinge of guilt about it, but it's overwhelmed by anticipation. Miles has barely touched you—there was that kiss outside the restaurant and some hand-holding in the taxi, but that's been all so far—which is somehow even more tantalizing than if he had his hands all over you. Every second he doesn't touch you makes you crave him more.

He leads the way to what is clearly the master bedroom. It contains a bed the size of a boxing ring, lots of mirrors, and a white leather love seat against one wall. At the touch of a button, music pipes in through invisible speakers and the lights dim just enough.

At last—he finally strokes his hand down your cheek and takes your chin again to kiss you. But he breaks the kiss off quickly, teasing you, forcing you to lean toward him, following his mouth with yours.

"Come here," you whisper, frustrated, reaching out and grabbing the back of his neck, pulling him toward you again. No longer tentative or teasing, he grabs you ferociously, tipping your head back, messing your hair, pressing your body against what feels like a rock in those expensively cut trousers. You arch against him, and he tugs at your hair. The difference between his usual suave style and the passion with which he's devouring you is hugely arousing, and it's clear from the erection you can feel pushing up against you that the feeling is entirely mutual.

Helena L. Paige

Then he steps back again, leaving you dizzy with lust and confusion, and strips off his shirt, revealing a torso that is clearly the product of long, disciplined hours in the gym.

"I want you to get that dress off. Now." It's a command, not a question, and it makes you pause.

"Okaaaay," you say, not moving, your stomach dipping a little. You're not sure about taking orders, even from a man who's used to hundreds of employees doing exactly as he says.

You stand staring at each other, and you sense that there's something he needs to tell you. His reticence is a dead giveaway.

"What is it?" you ask.

"I like to do things slightly differently."

"So you said."

"I have a box of tricks I want to share with you." Then, seeing your face, "It's not drugs or anything like that . . . but let me show you. It's easier than explaining."

Miles draws an unremarkable suitcase on wheels out from under the bed. It's black, and as to be expected, it looks extremely expensive. It also has a complicated-looking combination lock.

"Going somewhere?" you ask.

Your attempt at levity falls flat, as he completely ignores you. Oh god. You hope he's not going to pull out a gimp suit and ask you to pee on him, or anything like that.

He places the case on the bed and deals efficiently with the lock. You look on, curious and slightly wary.

"Come and stand here," he says quietly.

"Bossy much?" you say, remaining where you are.

"That's my job." His voice is still soft, but more insistent. Half of you is yelling to get the hell out of there, but the other half is curious. You take a step closer and peer into the suitcase.

You get a general impression of black leather goods laid along the bottom, and on top of that is a collection of different kinds of crops, whips, and other toys. There are paddles and beads, and are those handcuffs? You lean in gingerly for a closer look. There are also ostrich feathers and an assortment of vibrators, from a discreet little wand to one that is so big it's frankly terrifying. No way, you think, a girl has to draw the line somewhere. There is also an impressive assortment of condoms, including ribbed, studded, colored, and flavored ones.

"I warned you there would be adventure," he says. "I take it this is all new to you?"

"That's putting it mildly," you say. "I once had a boyfriend who blindfolded me with a silk scarf for fun, but we lost interest after I accidentally poked him in the eye while we were thrashing around."

"I'll completely understand if you'd like to leave now. I'll call a taxi for you—you only have to say the word."

You look at him uncertainly. He stands inches away from you, his bare chest rising and falling—otherwise perfectly controlled, the wildness of a few minutes ago brought to heel. There's no denying how attractive he is—your panties are in danger of melting.

"Let me be clear here," he says. "I could show you

Helena S. Paige

an entirely different kind of pleasure, and I think you know it. I can guarantee that you'd be completely safe at all times. You have my word on that. The idea is to take you somewhere entirely new."

You're torn. This is your chance to experiment with a little tasteful S&M, and you have to admit, you're just a tiny bit curious; it's what everyone's talking about these days. It helps that you're with one of the most powerful and sexy men in the city. He's experienced, he has all the props, he's discreet, and if that bulge in his pants is anything to go by, he really wants you. But the question is, do you really want him? And if so, do you want him badly enough to try something different? Or is it time to get out of there before things start to get really freaky?

🙈 If you decide to go for it, go to page 126.

🙈 If this just isn't your style and you want out of there, go to page 184.

a girl walks into a bar

❧ You decide to go for it

 "ALL RIGHT, SO IF, hypothetically speaking, I was to say yes . . ." you say, taking a step closer to him, so your bodies are now almost touching. Just a slice of air holds you apart.

"I don't think you'd be disappointed," he says, not moving to touch you.

"And you wouldn't hurt me?" you ask.

"Nothing that you couldn't handle. I think you'll discover that sometimes a little bit of pain can translate into a lot of pleasure. Hypothetically speaking, of course."

"Of course," you say. "But what if I want you to stop?"

"I'll stop the second you ask."

You raise an eyebrow at him, not convinced.

"We'll agree on a safe word, of course."

"A safe word?"

"Something you can say if you feel uncomfortable

at any point, that's a sign for the other person to stop what they're doing that instant. The words 'stop' and 'no' aren't always clear in the heat of the moment. Sometimes, when you get to the brink, 'stop' can mean 'go,' so we need to pick something absolutely clear, a word that couldn't possibly ever be confused with anything else. Something that we both agree signals 'Stop right this second!'"

This all feels slightly surreal. This is really happening—you're discussing safe words with a media magnate, who also happens to be your best friend's boss.

You're tempted to pick a silly word, like "jabberwocky" or "controlling bastard," but instead you say, "How about 'sea urchin'?"

He can't help smiling. "Well, technically that's two safe words, but 'sea urchin' it is. At least there's no way it's going to crop up in conversation and be mistaken for anything other than 'stop.'"

You nod, and with that decision made, he tugs you in for another kiss at last. Once you pull apart, he looks at you for a long moment. Then he changes pace: "Now get that dress off! I have something else in mind." And he lifts a gleaming black leather bustier with corset lacing out of the suitcase.

You stand there, not used to being given orders like this, trying to decide if you like it or not.

"I said, take it off," he growls.

Heat jolts through your body. You pull your dress up and off over your head and drop it to the ground. He reaches behind you and unsnaps your bra.

a girl walks into a bar

"All of it!" he says.

You swallow hard, then wriggle out of your G-string, covering yourself with your hands. But you're not stark naked for long; Miles helps you put the bustier on, turning you around and tugging the laces at your back so vigorously you yelp a little.

He rewards you for your obedience by first running a finger from the nape of your neck down your back through the lacing, and then stepping close behind you and nipping at the tops of your shoulders. The feel of his body against yours makes you want to turn, grab hold of him, and kiss him, and you start to move, but he grips your arms, holding you in place. "I didn't say you could turn around."

There's a row of mirrors on the wall-to-wall walk-in wardrobes, and you catch sight of yourself, wearing only your black high heels and the patent-leather black bustier, your hair tousled. The bustier makes your waist look tiny, and even you catch your breath at the sight. There's no denying it—the effect is hot. Behind you, you feel his breath in your ear as he whispers, "Choose a whip."

You gulp, nerves momentarily overcoming the heat in your pussy, but you peer into his box of tricks. There are some very businesslike-looking crops, a paddle that looks exactly like a Ping-Pong bat, another one like an oversize hairbrush that has short metal spikes protruding from one side, and also an old-fashioned wooden school ruler, complete with ink stains. You spot a cream-colored suede whip that ends in multiple tails of soft leather, knotted at the ends. It looks dainty and un-threatening, and you point to it. "That one."

He reaches for it, then leads you over to the love seat, which is probably worth more than all the furniture in your apartment.

"Stand in front of me," he says, sitting down on the edge of the seat.

You do as you're told, thinking that you might just be getting the hang of this. But you wish he would stop boss-ing you around and touch you already. You've had the bare minimum of actual physical attention since you got here, and now you really want it. Desire has been build-ing up inside you, need on top of need.

"Now turn around," he orders.

You twirl, showing off your bustier-improved body, and he whispers, "Perfect. You are very sexy, you know that? But you're also rather naughty, aren't you? I think I'm going to have to spank you."

Without warning, he grabs your wrists and clasps them together with one hand, then tugs sharply so that you lose your balance in your heels and tumble forward across his lap. You giggle as you fall, but then you gasp as he trails the loose ends of the little whip across your bottom and exposed lower back. The tickling sensation is deliciously erotic, and his erection is growing steadily beneath you. You feel the whip trailing along your naked buttocks and down your thighs to the back of your knees and then up again. The soft feel of it is de-lectable against your naked skin. The trailing whip dis-appears momentarily and you eagerly anticipate more.

a girl walks into a bar

You hear and feel a little slap as he lifts the whip and brings the suede strands down on your naked behind. It stings a little, but it's not unpleasant. He follows up by running a cool hand over your bottom, following the tracks of the fronds. The touch of his fingers on your naked skin immediately soothes away any memory of the sting of the whip.

Seconds later you feel his hand disappear, and the whip comes back down again, this time a little harder. The knotted ends catch you on the lower part of your bottom this time, and a few of them hit you on the back of your upper thighs. You suck in a breath, but immediately his hand is back on you, massaging your skin, taking away the sting. Then he rubs circles across your bottom before raising his hand and slapping it down onto your bare skin. You cry out at that one, more at the surprise of the flat-handed smack than the soft leather of the whip, and at the cracking sound than at the sting of it.

Again he rubs your buttocks, kneading your skin, his fingers briefly slipping between your legs—and you know how wet he's going to find you, the thought of which makes you even wetter.

After trailing a few fingers over your pussy, he returns his hand to your bottom and gives it another quick slap before again kneading the skin, which is now inflamed and sensitive to the slightest touch. You're starting to understand what this is about, a little bit of unexpected pain followed each time by the reward of touch turning the pain into something surprisingly

erotic. This is why your body is enjoying and respond-
ing to something you'd always thought you would find
completely unacceptable.

The sting of the last slap fades and is replaced with
goose bumps as you feel cool air across your bottom—he
must be blowing on you. Then his hand is withdrawn
again, and you brace yourself for whatever's coming, so
that this time you'll be prepared when his hand comes
down on you.

Then, crack! The whip comes down once more, and
this time it's not at all what you expect.

"Ouch! Dammit, that's sore!"

You thrash off Miles's lap and stagger to your feet,
rubbing your outraged ass with both hands.

"What do you think you're doing? That really hurt,
for fuck's sake!" you snarl.

For the first time, he looks nonplussed. "Safe word,"
he reminds you. "Use the safe word if you need to."

"The hell with your stupid safe word! That was sore
and you're not doing it again."

You glare at him, hands on your hips, your breasts
threatening to spill out of the bustier as your chest rises
and falls.

Miles is clearly discombobulated. He runs a hand
through his hair and the muscles in his arms flex. He
is so smoking hot, and he looks so disappointed, you
soften a little. Your ass may be throbbing, but you're still
as horny as hell, and you're not letting this opportunity
slip through your fingers. An idea occurs to you.

"Get over to the bed right now. I think you need a

a girl walks into a bar

taste of your own medicine," you say, standing up tall and pointing at the bed.

His eyes meet and hold yours for a moment, and you can practically hear swords clashing. You stare him down, and when he doesn't move, you take his hand and pull him roughly to his feet. Then you point at the bed again. "Now!" you say. "I mean it! Quickly!" Then you put a hand between his shoulder blades and shove him. To your astonishment, he goes like a lamb, and you're emboldened by his complicity. Maybe it's the leather bustier.

"Pants off and bend over the end of the bed. Do it now," you snap, diving into his suitcase. You know exactly what you want, and you smirk with satisfaction as your fingers close over it.

But your smile is replaced by an expression of awe as he steps out of his trousers and blindingly white shorts. He could double as a Calvin Klein model, except his cock is bigger and his six-pack more clearly defined than those of any male underwear model you've ever seen.

You stare at each other for a moment—then you watch almost in disbelief as this tall, muscled, powerful man walks meekly to the bed and bends, bracing his hands on the mattress, placing himself entirely at your mercy. Not that you intend showing him any—your bottom still stings.

You stand beside him and raise your weapon of choice—the schoolteacher's ruler—while admiring his firm, muscled buttocks. Then you bring your arm down with a satisfying whack. He jerks and groans, and you're a bit alarmed—have you been too enthusiastic? But as you stalk round him to check, you notice the effect on his already swollen cock as it rises still further.

You pause and then bring the ruler down again, this time slightly harder, and the second smack has the same effect. You remember how good it felt when he stroked your burning skin after hitting you, so you run your hand lightly over the area you smacked, feeling a small welt rising under your fingers, and you hear him groan at your touch. His skin is smooth and hot, the muscles twitching. You rub a little harder in small circles, the way he did, and when you think he'll least expect it, you quickly bring the ruler slapping back down on him again. Then you repeat your earlier actions, replacing the ruler with your fingers, kneading, massaging, and stroking his burning skin. At one point you slip your hand between his legs and cup his balls, squeezing them gently and feeling his entire body tense and shiver with excitement, then you slip your palm along his ever-hardening cock, but once only before you return your hand to his perfect behind.

By the time you've administered half a dozen blows, his penis is perpendicular and the big vein running underneath it is throbbing visibly. You've never seen such a perfect specimen, and it has you throbbing, too. You're finding all of this strangely exhilarating, and your pussy has big plans for that cock.

It's clear that Miles is as turned on by being bossed around as he was by doing the bossing, so it's time to dish out more orders, you think.

a girl walks into a bar

"Now, lie on the bed, on your back, with your arms above your head," you command, stepping back and thwacking the ruler into your palm a few times, your voice as crisp and assertive as a schoolmarm's. Yet again you're amazed when he complies without a murmur.

You investigate his suitcase once more and fish out the handcuffs. They look efficient, almost like the real deal—but instead of being lined with something cheesy like fake fur or leopard-print fabric, there's a deep layer of purple suede inside them. Like everything else in this home, they're the expensive kind. You snap one cuff around his wrist and the other around the bedpost, then put the key carefully on the far bedside table, so he can see you doing it—you do *not* want to lose that.

That takes care of one arm, but what to do about the other? You don't want him to have any control at all. You have an idea, and scoop up the shirt he stripped off earlier. Careless of the fine tailoring and with buttons popping everywhere, you use his bespoke shirt to tie his other arm to the corresponding bedpost.

Through all of this he lies still, watching your every move, groaning as you tug at his limbs, his rock-hard erection straining at the ceiling. You cannot wait to sit on it—your pussy is aching. You've already helped yourself to some intriguing-looking condoms from his treasure chest—they're black and covered with little rubber studs that look like they might feel incredible inside you.

Keeping the bustier and heels on, you climb on to the bed and straddle him. Looking down at him, you run your tongue over your lips and rotate your hips, swinging your pelvis just above his cock.

"Ask nicely," you say cheekily as he arches up at you frantically.

"Please," he begs, all restraint gone.

But you have another idea. He's been the one teasing you all night—now it's your turn. So you shuffle on your knees up toward his head, clambering over his torso until you're squatting over his chest.

"Miles," you inform him. "You did a very bad thing when you hurt me. So now it's payback time." And with that, you spread your thighs and sink down onto his face.

His tongue is ready for you and the next second, you're the one groaning. The soft, wet lips of your pussy meet his firm ones, which feel phenomenal against you. His tongue pushes firmly up into you, parting you, sliding in and up, making you cry out.

You rock gently as he moves his face slightly from side to side, tongue scorching you, licking your clit, pulling your lips into his mouth, tugging gently at them.

You hold on to the headboard with both hands and use it to lever yourself up and down, so you can alter the intensity of his attack. Until you realize that you're so close to coming, you either need to move away or surrender yourself to your orgasm.

You remember there's still that glorious penis waiting for you to enjoy, and there's no way you're missing out on that. So you brace yourself to pull away, and you

a girl walks into a bar

both moan as you slide away and down his body. You pause to roll the studded condom onto his magnificent erection, marveling at the smoothness of his heated and clean-shaven skin.

By now he's thrashing a little, so you administer a smart slap to his flanks. "Hold still!" you say, using your sternest voice. "I intend taking my time!"

You position yourself above his penis, and rub the head languorously against your opening, teasing both of you. You're so wet that you know he's going to slip inside you effortlessly, and you can't wait for it. His breath is coming in sharp gasps, and he's begging you again.

You clamp a hand over his mouth, and he nips your fingers, but the truth is you can't hold back any longer, and so you slide down the length of his thick cock with a drawn-out sigh of relief mingled with shock as he stretches your wet pussy to the limit. You bounce gently a few times, getting yourself accustomed to his size, and then you manage to take control again, aware that you need to keep a huge impending orgasm at bay. You sit still, gripping him tightly between your thighs.

"Look at me," you say, "I'm still in charge here. These are the rules. You can have four thrusts inside me. But that's it. Do you understand?" You can be disciplined and restrained, too, you decide.

He swallows. You're aware he has the perfect view of your breasts spilling out of the bustier, both nipples having escaped the low-cut cups.

Then you allow him to pound up into you four times, grinding hard back down on him each time,

before pulling yourself off and nipping at his neck. You can hear him panting. After a minute, you straddle him once more: "This time you can have ten thrusts," you tell him. "Only ten!"

He nods vigorously, clearly desperate for you. Slowly you lower yourself back down onto him, your eyes rolling back as he fills you up again, and then you count the thrusts you allow him out loud, one by one. By the time you reach the tenth thrust, it takes every inch of your control to slide off him again. And he groans again with lust and frustration.

You bite down on one of his nipples, running your hand up his rock-hard chest, the softness of his skin a contrast to the muscles underneath.

"I need you, now," he says in your ear, and the feeling is mutual.

"Fuck it," you say, your voice breathy, and this time when you straddle him, you brace your thighs and start to ride him, moving up and down slowly, with a circular swing to your hips, not counting the thrusts, just letting go and feeling the rhythmic pressure building inside you. The studs on the condom add a wicked new dimension to his penis, and you ride it as hard as you can, gripping his body between your knees, both of you rapt with pleasure.

You're the first to reach orgasm, in a series of noisy shudders, bracing your palms on his chest as you convulse, but you keep going and by the time he finally arches under you like a bow, you've come again, almost limp with the satisfaction of it.

a girl walks into a bar

It takes a long time before your breathing slows down, and for you to finally slide your sweat-slickened body off him and lie beside him. Then when you kiss, for what is astonishingly only the third time, it's long and gentle and slow.

You untie the shirt, so he has one hand free to stroke you with, but his other hand remains handcuffed to the bedposts, and he shows no desire to be released.

"Well, that certainly wasn't what I initially had in mind," he murmurs.

"Are you complaining?" you ask, pretending to reach for the ruler again. He laughs and pulls you back toward him. "I'd hate to have to gag you," you add, "especially considering the magic you can do with your mouth."

"So how did you like your first little foray into the dark side?" he asks, burying his face in your hair and kissing you on the top of your head.

"I may not have liked being on the receiving end as much as you'd hoped," you say. "But I have to admit I really enjoyed dishing it out."

"I enjoyed you dishing it out, too," he says, running the fingers of his available hand over your nipple.

You stretch and yawn. "It's getting late," you say. "I think I'd better get going."

"So soon? But I've still got a whole suitcase full of tricks."

"That's what I'm worried about." You swing your legs off the bed and stand up. The bustier is getting hot and uncomfortable, and you reach behind yourself and

Helena L. Paige

unlace it, making sure to face him so he can get a good look at you as you strip it off. You may as well continue to torture him—that seems to have been the overriding theme for the night—so you take your time putting your clothes back on.

Then you crawl back onto the bed and kiss him long and hard, loving the feel of his tongue taking control of your mouth. When you feel his free hand starting to snake under your dress, you pull away. He's insatiable.

"I think I'd better leave you restrained like this," you say, eyeing his handcuffed wrist. "To prevent you using your hands to try to persuade me to stay."

He pulls briefly against his bonds as he reaches for the key, which is only just out of reach on the bedside table. Then he lies back, and you're rewarded by the flare in his eyes.

"Sexy and smart," he says. "If I can't convince you with my hands, I don't suppose begging would persuade you to stay?"

"Thank you, but no." You bend over him and kiss that sensual mouth one last time.

"Wait!" His voice is hoarse. "There's one thing I want you to do for me before you go. Please."

You turn back toward the bed. Now what?

"There's a paddle in my case. I need you to get it out for me."

"Okay." You delve into his suitcase, a little puzzled. "Do you mean the one that looks like a Ping-Pong bat?"

"Yes. Have you found it?"

a girl walks into a bar

You fish it out and waggle it at him. "Here it is. What do you want me to do with it? Surely not more spanking?"

He shakes his head.

"What then?" You hold it by the handle and examine it more closely, trying to work out what other possible uses it might have.

"Here's a hint," he says. "Try the other way up."

You turn the paddle around and peer at the dildo-shaped handle, which you notice is slightly ridged—and suddenly you get it.

"You want me to put this . . . up there?" Your voice emerges as a shriek.

He nods.

You contemplate him, slowly slapping the paddle against your thigh. You're in unknown territory here, way beyond your comfort zone—surely this is a sign that it's long past time to leave? But then it's been a night of new adventures, so what have you got to lose by giving him a little parting gift?

❧ If you decide to accommodate his request, go to
page 141.

❧ If you just keep on going out the door, go to
page 142.

❧ You've decided to go along with Miles's request

🍹 Noooooooooooooooooooooooo! ARE YOU OUT of your mind? No way are you doing that!

❧ Go straight to page 142.

❧ You've decided to keep on going out the door

 "I'M SORRY, BUT MY work here is done. Good night, Miles, I'm sure you can manage on your own from here."

You shift the handcuff key a little closer to him so that, with a bit of effort, he'll be able to reach it. Then you walk to the door, swinging your hips. You'll never be able to look at a ruler in the same way again. Or play Ping-Pong, for that matter.

As you get into a taxi outside Miles's house, you marvel at the night you've had. Who would have thought when you were getting ready earlier this evening that this is where you'd end up? You yawn and stretch, completely satisfied. It's definitely home-time, you think, giving the taxi driver your address. Or there's that coffee shop close to your home; you could always ask to be dropped off there. Hot chocolate would be a decadent way to round off a decadent evening . . .

- ❧ If you go straight home, go to page 217.

- ❧ If you stop off at your local late-night coffee shop on your way home, go to page 242.

❧ You've decided not to go home with Miles

"You know what, it's getting late. I think I'd better call it a night, after all," you say, glancing at your watch. This man is magnetic, but perhaps it's better to keep him as a fantasy. Besides, he *is* Melissa's boss—you don't want things to get awkward.

Miles's shoulders sag briefly, but then he's back to his polite and composed self.

"Of course, I completely understand," he says. Then he slips his hand into his pocket and takes out his wallet. For one horrific moment you think he's going to offer you money. But instead he pulls out a business card.

"In case you're ever in the mood for something different," he offers with a small smile. "I'll get you a taxi."

Always so bossy, you think. Sexy at first, maybe, but now it's starting to wear a little thin. "I'll be fine, thanks.

I'm just going to head back inside to use the bathroom, and then I'll ask Katsuko to call me a taxi."

At that moment, a car pulls sleekly up to the curb in front of you, the back door perfectly aligned with where Miles is standing. Everything always seems to fall in this man's lap. Why should you do the same?

He kisses you on the cheek like a perfect gentleman, and before he's even closed the taxi door, you head back inside the restaurant.

Inside, it's almost empty; the lights are low, and there's no sign of Katsuko, so you wander back between the tables toward the sound of voices chatting and laughing.

You find three men sitting at a table at the very back of the restaurant, playing cards. You recognize two of them: the sushi chefs you were watching earlier. The third guy is also in a chef's uniform—he must work behind the scenes in the kitchen. You clear your throat, and all three heads turn toward you. The handsome one, who was doing the showy knifework earlier, leaps to his feet.

"Hello," he says, smiling, his voice slightly accented. "Can I help you? Did you forget something?" His eyes dart toward the counter where you and Miles were seated earlier.

"No, but I was wondering if it would be okay to stay here while I call a taxi and wait for it to arrive?"

"Of course," he says warmly. Then he cranes his neck, looking past you. "Is your boyfriend with you?"

"He's not my boyfriend. He's my best friend's boss."

a girl walks into a bar

The chef raises an interested eyebrow before reverting to courtesy mode.

"Of course. Make yourself comfortable." Then a thought strikes him. "You don't play poker, do you? One of the waiters, Takumi, is usually our fourth, but he had to go home early. We were going to call it a night, but maybe we can still play a couple of hands."

The other two guys look friendly, and one of them nods keenly, shuffles the deck of blue Bicycle cards and deals out a hand. You notice that he automatically deals you in, without waiting for an answer.

"What are you playing?" you ask.

"Texas Hold'em," says the handsome chef, holding one of the chairs out for you. "You know how to play? It's not difficult, I think you can pick it up fast."

"I used to play back in the day, but I'm probably really rusty."

"That's okay, Makio isn't much good, either," he jokes, and one of the trio snorts out a laugh. The one who must be Makio looks inquiringly at his friends—he probably doesn't speak much English.

You're no pro, but you've played before—sign of a wasted youth—so you're not a complete novice, and with luck you won't disgrace yourself. So should you stick around and play a couple of hands? They seem like nice enough guys, especially the head chef, and it doesn't hurt that he's so easy on the eye. But you don't want to intrude—what if they're only inviting you to be polite? Maybe you should just head home and unwind with a DVD and some popcorn.

- To stick around and play poker with the chefs, go to page 148.

- To go home to a DVD and some popcorn, go to page 238.

✌ You've decided to stick around and play poker

🍸 "Okay," you say. "I'll stay for a few hands, if you're sure I'm not intruding."

All three of them cheer as you take your seat at the table. "I'm Koji," says the head chef, and you shake hands, his fingers strong against yours. "That's Makio—he doesn't speak any English—and this is Benjiro. Watch out for him: he'll try and look at your cards."

Both men remain seated but bow their heads politely, and you offer a quick wave and introduce yourself. Koji slips behind the counter to fetch a cup for you and pours out some sake. They chat among themselves in Japanese as you take a sip.

"Big blind is two hundred, small blind is one hundred," Koji explains. He's referring to the automatic bets you have to make before playing each round. It's coming back to you, and you stack the chips Makio has pushed in front of you into some kind of order, then toss a few into the pot. You reach for your first two cards laying facedown on the table and look at them, careful to hold them as close to your body as possible. A jack and a seven.

Benjiro is dealing: he burns the top card in the deck, setting it aside, and then lays three community cards down in the middle of the table. You try to keep your face neutral as he turns over a four of clubs, a six of diamonds, and then another jack. That means you have two jacks. This could work, and your pulse quickens. You'd forgotten how much fun poker can be. You reach for your sake casually as the dealer burns another card and then turns the fourth communal card. It's another jack. It takes every ounce of self-control not to break into a huge grin.

Benjiro burns one last card, then turns the fifth and final community card, which is something useless, but it doesn't matter—what you've got is good enough to win, or at least not come last. You don't have to know a lot about poker to know how good a three of a kind is.

You're careful not to give anything away, betting conservatively through three or four rounds, until Makio eventually calls and you all turn your cards over on the table. Everyone leans forward to look at what's there, and it takes you a second to scan the cards, do the math, and realize that you've won. You want to punch the air and do a victory dance around the table as the three guys look at you in wonder.

"I thought you said you weren't very good!" Koji

a girl walks into a bar

says, beaming at you. Benjiro claps his hands, and Makio scratches his head.

"I'm not—it must be beginner's luck," you say, sweeping up the pile of chips you've won with no small amount of glee.

The next two hands are a bust, and you lose nearly all the chips you won in the first hand. You fold early in the following hand, and then lose to Benjiro, who manages to pull out two picture pairs.

But you find you're settling into the mood at the table and enjoying yourself. Who would have thought when you were dressing up for a girls' night out on the town that you would end up in a discreet Japanese restaurant, playing poker with three sushi chefs?

Your companions chat on, slipping seamlessly between English and Japanese, and Koji makes a point of translating as much of it as possible. You can't help sneaking sideways glances at him. He has jet-black hair cut short at the back, with a slightly longer fringe, along with thick, dark eyebrows, a long, aquiline nose, and full lips. If he wasn't a world-class sushi chef, you're sure he could cut it as a ramp model.

He makes a point of keeping your cup of sake topped up, and smiles every time you catch his eye. Once or twice you can feel his eyes on you when he thinks you're focusing on your cards, and it makes your heart rustle in your chest a little.

You play another two hands without winning. And then on the next hand, something miraculous happens: you get a nine and a king of clubs in the initial draw,

then Makio, who's dealing, draws a ten, jack, and queen of clubs as the community cards. Your eyes widen—you know that the hand you've been given is just about the Grand Prix of poker hands. You play it cool, trying to remember everything you've ever heard about bluffing, so as not to tip off the guys. You bet as cautiously as you can while still keeping the pot growing.

Benjiro folds almost immediately, followed two rounds later by Makio, who shakes his head and drops his cards facedown. You and Koji face off, and you can see by the glint in his eye that he also has good cards. You scramble to remember the rules, trying to guess what cards he would need to beat your hand, but you're pretty sure yours can beat any competition. You pretend to weigh up your options, fiddling with your chips and acting conflicted about whether to bet more.

There are another few rounds of betting, with both your piles of chips dwindling dangerously, neither of you wanting to be the first to concede.

"All in," Koji says at last with a wicked grin, surveying the small pile of chips remaining in front of you and sweeping his every last chip into the middle of the table. Then he calls, turning his cards over and laying them down flat on the table. He has three aces. It's good, but it's not good enough, and you keep your face blank while your heart thumps, and the guys all lean in to get a closer look, oohing and aahing at his hand.

Your expression innocent, you fan your cards out faceup, so everyone can see what you've got.

Both Benjiro and Makio whoop, and Koji, who was

a girl walks into a bar

about to sweep up all the chips, assuming he'd won, looks at the cards, up at you, and back at the cards again.

"What!" he says, his face comic with shock. "No way!"

You smile casually, as if you pull royal flushes out of nowhere and bankrupt your opponents every day of the week.

Benjiro rattles something off in Japanese and Makio bursts out laughing. You can tell they're teasing Koji, who laughs good-naturedly.

"You got me!" he says as Benjiro and Makio gather their bits and pieces. "They want to know if you'll come back next week?" he goes on, and the two men smile at you. "They say anyone who beats me is a friend of theirs!" Everyone laughs, and as the guys count out their remaining chips and finish their drinks, you excuse yourself to go to the ladies' room.

WHILE YOU'RE WASHING YOUR hands and fixing your hair, you visualize Koji at the table, the muscles in his forearms rippling, and you see your cheeks flush in the mirror. You picture those lips, imagining them pressed against yours—you're sure they would feel soft as pillows and taste like a ripe piece of fruit. As you dry your hands in the compact hand dryer, which is toasty warm, you notice a condom dispenser bolted to the wall next to the sink. And it gets your mind wandering beyond kissing. You imagine what Koji would be like in bed. You've already seen proof of his dexterity this evening.

If his tongue skills are anything like his knife skills, he's sure to be pretty spectacular, you think, then blush at your thoughts.

But the condom dispenser is giving you ideas, and on impulse you dig around in your handbag for a few coins, which you place in the slot. Then you turn the knob, and a condom in a purple sleeve slips out and into your hand. You drop it into your bag. You're not quite sure why you're doing it, but you tell yourself a girl can never be too safe.

BACK IN THE RESTAURANT, Koji is alone at the table, idly shuffling the cards.

"Did the boys go?" you ask.

"Yes, they said to say goodbye and thank you for the game," he says. "They also said to tell you same time, same place next week. They're hoping they can replace Takumi with you—you're much nicer to look at than he is, and we suspect he cheats."

You smile at the buried compliment. "I'm sorry I didn't get to say goodbye. I really liked them," you say, a little disappointed that the night has come to an end.

"They're good guys," Koji says. "Both of them have been with me right from the beginning; Makio is my cousin."

"This is your place?" you ask, impressed.

"Katsuko is my sister—we run it together," he says.

"It's phenomenal," you say. "Best sushi I've ever had. Except for the eyeballs!"

Koji throws his head back and roars with laughter. "You did ask for it!"

You shake your head at the memory. "Thank you for inviting me to play with you," you say, reaching for your bag and phone, intending to call a taxi.

"You're not leaving yet, are you?" He looks disappointed. "I was hoping you would at least give me a chance to win some of my money back."

You take a long look at him, your body stirring at the thought of staying for a more intimate game with him. You curb the urge to lean forward and run your fingers through his fringe.

"Why not? Just a few more rounds, then I'll call a taxi."

You sit down again, just the two of you with the whole restaurant to yourselves. The lights are low, and your breath quickens as he deals out the cards. You take a big sip of sake—you need a little Japanese courage.

Koji beats you in the first hand, and in the next one, too. But it's worth losing to see those delectable lips turning up at the corners every time he wins.

Next it's your turn to deal, and as you shuffle the cards, you have a bold idea. Even you are a little surprised to hear the words coming out of your mouth: "Why don't we raise the stakes a little?"

"What, up the ante?" he asks, raising a thick eyebrow.

"Yes, why not?"

"What do you want to up it to?" he asks, and you know you're both thinking the same thing—it's just a matter of who's going to say it first.

You take the plunge. "How about for every loss, we take off an item of clothing?"

"I thought you'd never suggest it!" he says. "But your beginner's luck can't last forever, you know. I plan on beating the pants off you!"

"We'll see about that," you say. Then you deal the cards quickly, hoping he won't notice that your hands are trembling. You beat him in the first hand, with nothing fancier than a pair of jacks—pure luck of the draw. He smiles and sheds his chef's coat without any comment, standing up and making a show of slipping each of the white buttons out of their holes, not taking his eyes off you for a second. He's not wearing a shirt underneath, and you marvel at his smooth, sculpted chest. Each of his abdominal muscles is so clearly defined, it's as if he's carved them with one of his knives. You stare openly—at this point you'd no sooner take your eyes off him than fly yourself to the moon.

Next it's his turn to deal. You do a quick garment count as he shuffles: you have your dress, your heels, and your bra and underwear—just the four items. While he still has his shoes, socks, trousers, and a pair of underpants to go. So you're even for now. Once again, you thank your lucky stars you wore your lacy G-string tonight—Koji is right, your winning streak can't go on forever.

You manage to sneak through the second hand with two low pairs, but his pair of tens is no match, and he sheds his shoes.

You lose the next hand, and slip out of your shoes, doing it slowly and deliberately to tease him after the

a girl walks into a bar

show he made of shedding his coat. He laughs as you do it, filling both your cups with more sake.

Your head buzzes with desire, the urge to reach over and run a hand across his chest mounting with every passing second. Then, much to your delight, Koji manages to lose the next two hands in quick succession, and you wonder if he's losing deliberately. First he sheds his socks, then he's forced to stand and drop his trousers to the floor. This leaves him in nothing but a pair of white briefs, luminescent against the tan of his skin. You gaze at his smooth, taut thighs, and you can't help but notice his generous erection growing by the second.

"I think I might have a hustler on my hands," he says, teasing to break the sexual tension rising like smoke between you. "It's a good thing we're only playing for clothes—if it was money, you'd be taking me to the cleaners."

"I'm just a lucky girl," you say, holding his eyes and smiling slowly. Who knew poker could be so rewarding? "This is better than winning money, if you ask me. It's your turn to deal," you say, handing him the pack. His fingers brush your hand as he takes the cards from you, and the tension ratchets up a notch.

He shuffles the cards, studying you closely.

"What are we playing for this round?" you ask, your voice husky.

He stops shuffling for a second. "How about winner takes all?" he says.

You nod, desire a slow burn in your chest and your pussy. He deals and you reach for your cards, almost

Helena L. Paige

afraid to look. Koji lays out the rest of the cards, and you keep checking your hand, hoping some valuable combination will materialize before your eyes, but you've got nothing. When it's time to call, the only flush is on your cheeks as you lay out your hand. Koji whoops as he lays out his cards, and you see he has two fours. Hardly the best hand in the world, but it's certainly enough to beat you.

"At last!" he shouts, grinning broadly. "I win!"

"Yup, and winner takes all," you say. With that, you stand up and slip your hands under your dress. Moving slowly and teasingly, you take hold of your panties on either side of your hips and pull the lace down off your thighs, past your knees to your ankles, and then you step carefully out of each leg.

Koji watches your every move, his eyes wide with desire, his erection now straining impressively under the tight fabric of his underpants. Once you've dropped your G-string on the floor, you step over to where he's sitting, almost naked on his chair, and you sit astride him, feeling the warmth of his body, and beneath you the power of him pressing hard against you, through the only item of clothing he has left on. He wraps both his arms around you and kisses you, and you were right about his lips, they're so full and soft that your lips sink into them. His tongue touches yours, and it tastes like sake. As you kiss you can feel him grinding up against your naked and very wet pussy, and you grind back down on him.

He drops his warm mouth on to one side of your

a girl walks into a bar

neck and runs his hand up and down the other side, his fingers deft and strong.

And then he's kissing you again, and he slips the straps of your dress and bra down and takes the weight of one of your breasts in his hand, kneading it gently. Then he takes one of your taut nipples in his mouth, teasing it with a very agile tongue. He returns to kiss your mouth, and while he's doing that his hands move lightly to your thighs under your dress, stroking and massaging the flesh, shifting further and further up until the thumbs of both his hands are rubbing between your legs, massaging your inner thighs and at last finding your slit and stroking it, too.

You close your eyes and try to remember to breathe as waves of pleasure spread through your body. You drop your hands down to free his hard, throbbing cock from the restraint of his underwear, and as you run your fingers over the length of it, you're astonished at how silkily smooth it is—his skin is so soft to the touch, it's like velvet.

"I never thought I'd be so happy to literally lose the shirt off my back," Koji murmurs. "Even though I lost, I still won," he says, before tilting his head back down and kissing you deeply again.

Not speaking, you reach back toward the table for your purse, fishing for the condom you bought earlier. You hold it out to Koji and watch him open the wrapping and stretch the condom over himself. Then he kisses your neck again, and you run your nails gently

over the top of his back, then his shoulders and up his neck and into his hairline, alternating soft, tickling scratches with slightly sharper, more needy ones. Then you run your nails back down his neck and his shoulders, being sure to cruise the tender, sensitive area below his arms, down his sides, and you hear him gasp audibly at the feel of your nails.

Then, unable to wait any longer, you take his sheathed cock in your hand and slide down onto it slowly, your breath catching as he fills you entirely. And then you rock backward and forward very slowly, getting accustomed to the size and shape of him inside you. The feeling is so good it's almost unbearable, and he gets the message from your moans, rocking his hips back and forth in tandem with yours. Slowly you speed up, never bouncing, only ever rocking, and it's like he's massaging your pussy from the inside. Your eyes shut tight, you clasp his shoulders, and then he kisses you with such abandon that you forget where you are for a moment.

And then you don't want to hold back anymore, so you rock faster, and an intense orgasm washes through you, his lips still pressed against yours, his tongue winding around yours, breathing the same breath. And you can feel your pussy clenching and unclenching around his cock, as you scratch your nails hard down his back, and the sensation takes him over the edge, and he wraps both arms around your back as he comes, squeezing your body tightly as he cries out in pleasure.

a girl walks into a bar

Flooded with the relief of your orgasm, you drop your forehead down onto that perfect silky shoulder, both of you fighting to get your breath back.

"How about another round—double or quits?" he says when he can finally speak again. You can't help but giggle into the softness of his neck.

LATER, AFTER YOU'VE BOTH won one more time, he leads you through the restaurant back to his kitchen. He's wearing just his underpants, and you've slipped into his oversize chef's jacket, the sleeves rolled up to fit you. He brews up a pot of green tea, and you sit on a high stool at the counter, blowing on your cup to cool it, enjoying watching his deft, sure movements as he wipes down each of his knives and packs them away into their leather carry-case.

He feels your eyes on him, reaches into one of the fridges, and pulls out a perfect red radish. Then he selects a small, lethally sharp–looking knife, and sets about the radish, his hands moving so quickly they're a cartoon blur. Seconds later he holds the radish out to you—he's carved it into a perfect red rose. You laugh, touched at the sweetness of the gesture, and he puts away the last knife before giving you one more gentle kiss.

You stroll back into the restaurant on rubber legs, and he turns off the lights and locks up while you call a taxi. It's definitely time to head home—and with a smile on your face. Your only decision is whether to stop

Helena L. Paige

by your late-night coffee shop on the way, for a celebratory hot chocolate.

🙢 To go straight home, go to page 217.

🙢 To go home via your local late-night coffee shop, go to page 242.

a girl walks into a bar

❧ You've decided to get a ride home in the sports car with the bodyguard

 You watch as the George Clooney look-alike drives off in the taxi. He certainly was charming, but tonight is definitely a night for racing around in a sports car.

"So, you ready to go?" the bodyguard asks in that deep brown molasses voice, slipping his phone back into his pocket.

"Everything okay?" you ask, indicating the phone.

"Yeah, all good. Just a little misunderstanding. So, shall we?" He grins and gestures at the car.

You hesitate. "My mother always told me never to accept rides from strangers."

"Doesn't the fact that I was a cop make you feel any better?"

"A little bit, but how do I know you were a good cop, not a bad cop?"

He smiles and you notice that he has dimples, not to mention the most perfect white teeth, both of which help to soften his strong jaw.

"To be honest, back in the day, sometimes I had to be a little bit of both. But tonight I promise you'll only get good cop."

You run through your options. You wouldn't normally get into a car with a complete stranger, but this guy is hardly a *complete* stranger, is he? First of all, you feel safe with him—and your instincts are usually good; second, he's Charlie Dakar from the Space Cowboys' personal bodyguard—it's his job to look after people; and third, this isn't just a car, it's a limited-edition, supercharged, incredibly rare classic. Surely different rules apply in this kind of situation?

You stroke the car's smooth, eye-candy curves. You can't help wondering what your car-mad ex would say if he knew you were contemplating a ride in one of these. Or what Melissa would say if she knew what you were planning, and who the car belonged to.

"Here, give me your phone," says the bodyguard, holding out his hand.

Curious, you hand over your cell. He walks around the front of the car and takes a photograph with it. Then he comes back and hands you the phone.

"There you go," he says. "Send that shot to a friend, and tell them who you're with. That way, if anything happens to you, they'll know where to start looking."

You examine your phone and see he's taken a pho-

a girl walks into a bar

tograph of the license plate (which is, embarrassingly, SEXGD 1). You have to remind yourself that it's not his car. If it was, all bets would be off—forget never getting into a car with a strange man, no self-respecting woman should ever get into a car with an arrogant personalized license plate.

"Wow, that's not a bad idea," you say. You fire off a quick text to Melissa and explain what you're up to, and to let her know that you'll message her again in a couple of hours to let her know you're okay.

The bodyguard opens the passenger door for you. You slide into the bucket seat, enjoying the feel of the soft, cool leather against your skin. There's not a single straight edge in the car's interior: every surface is curved and sleek, and the dashboard would look perfectly at home in a space shuttle.

The bodyguard closes your door and then goes around to the driver's side. He takes off his jacket and drops it onto the back seat, giving you the opportunity to inspect arm muscles that strain at the sleeves of his shirt. You were worried that he'd barely fit inside the car, but the interior is larger than you were expecting, and while he fills the seat, there's more than enough room above his head for comfort.

As he slots his seat belt into its socket, his fingers briefly brush your thigh. Neither of you says anything, but your skin smolders where he touched you. You catch a trace of his scent, a masculine woody smell that melds perfectly with the car's leather, and for a second you're

Helena L. Paige

reminded of Mr. Intense. But sitting here, next to this bear of a man, your body tingling with anticipation at the thought of shooting through the night in a super-charged high-performance machine, you don't feel a shred of regret.

You tell him your address, and he programs it into the car's onboard GPS. "You mind if we take the high-way?" he asks. "It's a bit of a detour, but at this time of night, with no cars on the road, it might be more fun."

You take a second to consider. "Okay. But if it looks like you're trying to abduct me, then I'm going to yank up the hand brake. At full speed. And you know what that means." You smile sweetly at him and he chuckles, a deep rumble.

"Don't worry, you're safe with me, I promise," he says, turning the key in the ignition. The car purrs, and when he guns the engine, making it roar, you can feel its power thrumming through your body. He presses a button and the sunroof whirrs open. You look up at the stars.

He eases out of the parking spot, then lets the car idle. "Ready?" he asks.

You open your mouth to reply, but all you can do is yelp, exhilarated, as he slams his foot on the accelera-tor and the car springs forward, the g-force pushing you back in your seat. As the speed increases, you let out a laugh and, clearly encouraged, he tears through the streets, expertly running through the gears, his muscles rippling with every gear-change. He flicks on the car's

a girl walks into a bar

surround-sound system, and you lean back and relax into the soft leather, the thud of the music and the throb of the powerful engine pulsing through your body. You can tell how comfortable he is behind the wheel; he was made for this car, and you can't help thinking that you were, too.

The engine roars as you fly through the deserted late-night city, the music pumping and the wind tearing through your hair. He swings onto the highway, barely slowing around the corner, and you feel the slight heart-stopping weightlessness of a skid before the car regains traction again. He's clearly showing off, putting the car through its paces. The car eats up the miles, and you mostly have the late-night highway to yourself. You can feel your heart beating in your throat, and when you look across at him, the exhilaration on his face matches exactly what you're feeling.

Then, with no warning, and much to the distress of the GPS, which starts recalculating immediately, he yanks the steering wheel hard right and takes an exit, the car now practically sideways. He straightens it effortlessly and shoots down the ramp. "Sorry!" he yells over the music. "I can feel my phone vibrating, just got to check my messages."

Back in the city, he pulls to a sharp stop outside a late-night corner store. You can't help grabbing his leg to brace yourself as the car screeches to a halt. Embarrassed, you snatch your hand back. But it's nice to know you were right—if his thigh is anything to go by, his body *is* pure muscle. He turns off the ignition and you can finally hear yourself think again.

"Sorry," you say. You're certain your cheeks are flushed with adrenaline, and your hair must look pretty wild from being whipped around by the night air.

"Sorry for what?" he says, digging his buzzing phone out of his pocket.

"Grabbing your leg."

"There's nothing quite like it, hey?" he says, and you notice that his face is also flushed.

"The car or your leg?"

He laughs, then scrolls through his phone. "My guy's ready for me," he says, looking a little disappointed. "I suppose I'd better take you home first."

You're disappointed, too. You spot a couple of teenagers shooting the car admiring looks before disappearing into the store.

"Or . . ." he says, leaving it hanging.

"Or what?"

"You could come with me if you like. It's just a quick detour. Then I can take you straight home afterward."

"What exactly does this 'run' entail?"

"I told you, nothing illegal. I've just got to pick something up for Charlie. It won't take long. And," he says with another smile, "we can take the highway again."

You think about it. You definitely haven't had your fill of this car yet, let alone this man. But what on earth is he up to? Maybe you should just play it safe and go back to the bar for a nightcap.

a girl walks into a bar

If you decide to accompany him on his mystery errand, go to page 169.

If you ask him to take you back to the bar, go to page 186.

Helena L. Paige

✥ You decide to go with the bodyguard on his mysterious errand

🍸 "I'LL COME WITH YOU on one condition," you say. "No—two."

"Go on. But let's not forget who's doing who the favor here."

"One: that you're not about to get me involved in anything that might kill me or land me in jail. Two: that you let me drive." You mentally add up how much you've had to drink. It was really just that one glass of sparkling wine. You should be okay.

"No way," he says. "Absolutely not. Under no circumstances."

"Why not? You chicken?"

"I'm not chicken! Do you know how much this car is worth? It's a classic."

"I know exactly how much it's worth," you lie.

"I don't mean to sound patronizing . . . but do you

really think you could handle a high-performance machine like this?"

"Why don't we find out?" You smile at him sweetly.

He sighs.

You bat your eyelashes in a parody of a flirt. "Pretty
please?"

He stares at you, and you can see him turning the
idea over in his head.

"Look, just give me a quick go. I'll drive from here to
that streetlight two blocks away, and if you don't think
I can manage this car, I'll jump right out and let you
drive again."

He still looks unsure.

"I won't even argue. If you say you want the car back,
I'll just hand her straight back to you, Scouts' honor,"
you say, fabricating some kind of salute. "Did I tell you
I used to be a Girl Scout?"

He sighs again. Then he narrows his eyes at you as if
he's weighing the consequences. "Okay, but my turn to
lay down a couple of ground rules."

"Ooooh, bossy, I like it."

"I'm being serious! No grinding the gears, they can
be a little stiff. And easy on the clutch."

"Deal."

"No running any red lights."

"Yes, officer."

"And you're never to let on to Charlie or anyone else
that I let myself be talked into this."

"My lips are sealed."

"If you break any of those rules, then I'll have to get my guns out."

Oh shit. "You have guns?"

"Sure." He lifts both arms, pulls the bicep in his right arm, then the bicep in the left arm. "This one, and this one."

They're huge. You laugh and he grins back at you. "I can't believe I let you talk me into this," he says as he hauls his bulk out of the driver's seat. "I really hope you know what you're doing."

You run around the car to take the driver's seat before he changes his mind, pausing to pull off your shoes. If you're going to put this beast through its paces, heels will definitely be a hindrance. As soon as he slides into his seat, you drop your shoes on his lap.

"Now I'm really beginning to regret this," he says.

The seat is pushed so far back to accommodate his size that you can barely touch the pedals with your toes. He leans across you to help you adjust the seat, his arm pressing against your breasts.

"Sorry," he says.

"Don't be."

The air between you is charged all of a sudden, and you think if you pretend to struggle with the seat belt, maybe he'll lean over you again. Then you take a deep breath and shake off the feel of his arm; you need to concentrate on getting your bearings. In seconds you have the gears, indicators, and rev counter placed, and you're confident you know what you're doing.

a girl walks into a bar

The bodyguard places a hand on your leg, to get your attention. You like the way it feels—reassuring *and* sexy. He looks at you earnestly and nervously: "Promise you won't crash?"

"I promise," you say. "I promise on both of our lives I will not crash this phenomenally expensive, limited-edition monster of a sports car."

"And remember what I said about the gears."

"I remember."

"And the other rules."

"Okay, okay. Can we go now?"

He sighs once more and removes his hand. "What the hell. Go for it."

Fresh adrenaline floods your system as you turn the ignition and feel the engine roar in response. You turn off the GPS so there are no distractions. It's way more exciting now that you're in the driver's seat. You take a deep breath, release the hand brake, drop the car smoothly into gear, and put your foot down on the accelerator.

"Easy, tiger!" you hear him shout as you surge forward. You handle the steering wheel, going just fast enough to get a rush, but not so fast that you terrify the pants off him. You drive the two hundred yards in seconds, then execute a perfectly polite stop directly in line with the promised streetlight. Not a stall, not a judder, not a single ground gear. You even impress yourself.

You look across at him demurely. He's clutching his seat with both hands, and looking at you in awe.

"I was not expecting that!"

"Happy? Can we go now?"

He nods and grins, and you rev the accelerator quickly, check your mirrors, and put your foot down. When you're sure he's not looking, you flip the traction control off. This is going to be fun. You wait until the rev counter reaches the red zone, then drop the clutch and floor the accelerator.

"Holy fuck!" he shouts as the car leaps forward.

"There was nothing in your rules about not doing a wheel spin," you shout above the thunder of the engine. The car is superresponsive, and as you turn the corner at the end of the street, the back slides out. You tweak the wheel to compensate, then decide to slow down and turn the traction control back on before you give your passenger a heart attack.

"Okay, okay, you've made your point!" he yells.

"Scared yet?"

"Shit, you really can drive."

You drop into third, check that the junction ahead is clear, and gun the engine again. "Thanks."

"Where did you learn how to do that? Are you Lewis Hamilton's sister or something?"

"I wish. It's all down to Grand Theft Auto."

"Grand Theft Auto? The Xbox game?"

"Kidding," you lie.

He laughs, and you can feel him checking you out again, his view of you clearly different this time. You're aware that the skirt of your dress has ridden up your thighs as you worked the clutch and accelerator, but you don't move to pull it down.

a girl walks into a bar

"So," you ask, "where are we headed?"

"South. But how about we take the long way around?"

You share another grin. Then you press your foot down.

As you slide onto the highway, letting the speedometer inch even higher, you can feel him relaxing next to you. He instructs you to take an exit that leads into one of the more expensive suburbs in the city, then he leans back and turns the music up. You're curious about your destination, but he wouldn't be able to hear any questions over the roar of the engine, the beat of the track, and the whoosh of the wind, and you wonder if this is why he's cranked up the volume.

Still, you're pleased he isn't trying to interfere with your driving. It feels good to be trusted, and even when you let the car have its head, pushing it to a speed that makes you feel wonderfully reckless, he merely looks at you and smiles. When you smile back, he lays one arm lightly along your headrest, and places a hand gently on the back of your neck, massaging the column of nerves just under your hairline with his fingers. As he touches you, you drop your shoulders and feel the tension leak away from your neck. There's a part of you that wishes this would never end: his strong hands on your skin, your foot pressing against the accelerator, the empty city roads around you, the night sky above you, and the feel of the powerful engine throbbing below you, up through your seat.

All too soon he removes his hand from the back of your neck, and you miss it instantly. He indicates that

Helena S. Paige

you should pull into a multistory parking garage alongside a towering glass building. The parking garage appears to be deserted, all the gates raised.

You pull the car to the curb and turn to glare at him. "Seriously? A deserted parking garage?"

He shrugs.

"I thought you said you weren't doing anything sketchy? Because this location is a massive 'doing something sketchy' cliché."

"Trust me."

You hesitate. You're in the driver's seat. In a worst-case scenario, you can just get out of there—put the pedal to the metal and drive away. You can always return the car to the bar and its rightful owner later.

You take a deep breath, rev the engine again, and shoot into the entrance, concentrating on swinging the car around the multiple ramps as fast as you can.

The bodyguard instructs you to head to the roof level, which also seems to be deserted. All you can see from here is the night sky and the city for miles in every direction. He gestures for you to hang a left. You drive slowly across the deserted concrete landscape, slamming on your brakes when a pair of headlights flash in front of you. You can make out the shape of a top-of-the-range white BMW, which is parked fifty yards or so away.

"I'm not going any farther," you say.

The bodyguard puts his hands up in a gesture of defeat. "Okay, okay." He opens the passenger door and heaves himself out. "I'll be right back."

You watch him sauntering toward the Beemer, then

a girl walks into a bar

you execute a quick three-point turn in case you have to get out of here in a hurry—you've seen scenes like this in gangster movies and anything could happen, so you leave the car in gear. You can hear your heart beating hard and fast in your ears, and you're clutching the steering wheel so tightly, your fingernails are digging into the leather. This must be how getaway drivers feel waiting outside the bank for the robbers to come charging out.

You glance into the rearview mirror, watching the bodyguard lean in through the front window of the darkened BMW. He's too far away for you to make out exactly what's going on over there. You force yourself to remain calm, but all you can picture is the interior of a prison cell. You're going to kill him for roping you into this.

The transaction takes less than a minute, and then the bodyguard is walking casually back to the car, both his hands in his pockets. The BMW comes to life and crawls across the rooftop, speeding up and turning on its lights as it hits the down-ramp.

The bodyguard slides into the car, closing the door and pulling on his seat belt. "All right?" he asks.

"Now that," you say, not bothering to hide your anger, "was sketchy as hell! You lied to me."

He upends a paper bag into your lap. "See for yourself."

Expecting to see a bag of white powder or something equally dubious spilling out of it, you're shocked into silence as you look down at a plastic packet containing several bright blue pills. You recognize them instantly. *"Viagra?"*

He nods. "Viagra. The guy in the BMW owns the late-night pharmacy on Kent Street."

"Viagra? That's not illegal. Why all the secrecy?"

"Imagine if the press found out that a couple of the boys in the Space Cowboys have a little trouble getting it up. It's not very rock star, is it?"

You laugh. "Nope, not very rock star at all. I must say, now I'm really glad I didn't go with Charlie."

"You don't know the half of it."

You look over at him, serious for a second. "I'm sorry I didn't trust you."

"No worries." He smiles, and those incongruous dimples pop out again. "Listen . . ." he says reluctantly. "This has been fun, but I'd better get this stuff back to the boys. Where do you want me to take you?"

You run through your options. After all this, do you really want to go straight home? You could head back to the bar for a last drink. But then again, you like the idea of being driven home in style.

❧ If you ask him to drop you off at home,
   go to page 178.

❧ If you ask him to take you back to the bar,
   go to page 186.

❧ You've asked him to take you home

 "OKAY IF I HAVE my car back now?" he rumbles with a grin.

You make a show of being deeply reluctant, but the truth is, as much as you loved handling the beast, you're looking forward to sitting back and watching those muscles work their magic through the gears again.

You swap places and laugh as he's forced to readjust the seat back to its full extension. You tell him your address again, and he programs it back into the car's GPS.

"Thank you for taking me with you," you say as he effortlessly guides the car down the curves of the parking garage's ramps. "It was a hell of a rush."

"Thank you for coming with me instead of going with Charlie," he says. "I don't think I've ever seen anyone turn him down before."

"Oh, I wouldn't be so sure. If he needs Viagra, then I'd say he knows all about turning down."

It's a pretty pathetic crack, but the bodyguard slaps the steering wheel and laughs, his dimples dipping into his cheeks. You drop your hand on to his leg again, squeezing it lightly. Maybe it's all the adrenaline of driving such a fast car and the aftereffects of the "deal" still pumping through your body, but touching him comes naturally.

In response, he keeps one hand on the steering wheel and drops the other one onto your leg, just above the knee, your arms crossing. His hand is strong and cool on your leg, and you feel wild and daring. Your pussy surges with desire, and you find yourself wanting more. So you remove your hand from his knee and place it on top of his hand on your leg. Then you slowly slide his hand up your thigh.

He takes his eye off the road and glances at you briefly. You give him your most dazzling smile, then slide his hand even higher up your thigh, so that it slips under the hem of your dress. He shoots a grin at you, then focuses back on the road, not taking his eyes off it. He slows the car a little and then, still in perfect control, he slides his hand even higher.

You part your legs and breathe deeply, thoroughly relishing the feel of his fingers on you. He massages your thigh lightly as he moves his hand higher and higher.

The four-lane highway is deserted. You, the bodyguard, and the sports car own the road.

a girl walks into a bar

You open your legs as wide as they will go in the seat and lean back as far as you can, angling your pelvis so that he has access to the very core of you. As his fingers touch the lace of your G-string, you know he must be able to feel how wet you are, and you watch a small smile creep across his face.

He flicks on the cruise control and slips his fingers under the lace of your tiny purple panties, running them gently through your bush. Then his fingers stroke up and down the length of your slit, sliding between the lips. You push your pelvis against his hand, eager for him to keep going. After a couple of moments teasing you, he slips a finger inside and you close your eyes and sigh. Within seconds he has located your clit and rolls one finger around the sensitive spot, while another finger slips in and out of you. You push your feet down hard against the floor of the car and brace yourself as he continues to rub against you. Your breath becomes more and more frantic, and you can't stop yourself from thrusting your hips upward.

Maybe it's because you know you'll probably never see this guy again, or because you're in a collector's-edition sports car, or because you can see the stars above, but you feel completely uninhibited. You grab one of your breasts, feeling how hard your nipple is. Then you lift one of your bare feet onto the dashboard in front of you, and he slips one more finger inside you, filling you up, still rubbing slow circles around your clit. The wind rushes through your hair and you can't help moaning. Then he speeds up his fingers bit by bit, working them

Helena L. Paige

inside you faster and faster, and you clutch the sides of your seat with both hands. Then, with the feel of expensive leather and the vibration of the engine beneath you, and his fingers inside you, you cry out as you come, shuddering with your head thrown back against the headrest, your eyes shut tight.

As you slowly come back down to earth, you feel him slip his fingers out of you, but he still holds on to the top of your thigh with his hand, massaging the flesh gently, and you're sure he can feel the tremble in your legs.

You eventually open your eyes as you feel the car slowing down, and discover that you're on a quiet, leafy side street. It takes you a moment to recognize that it's your road. The bodyguard pulls up outside your apartment block and turns off the car engine. Then he leans in and kisses you, your teeth clashing as your tongues entwine. Eventually he leans back, his eyes gleaming.

"What a ride," you say as you finally manage to catch your breath, feeling bashful and shocked at your own behavior. What on earth got into you? You sit up a little straighter, tug your skirt down, and try to smooth your hair, which is wild and knotted.

He senses the shift in your mood, and leans toward you. "Hey, come here," he says in his deep growl, lifting you easily out of your seat and pulling you into his lap. He holds you and strokes your hair out of your face, pinning it behind your ears. "Don't be shy, that was amazing," he says. "You're amazing."

You blush. "I'm not normally so . . . so . . . so . . ."

He smiles and kisses you deeply again, so you no

longer have to search for words. You wrap your arms around his neck and kiss him back. This time, the kiss is less urgent, and his tongue is soft and gentle. You imagine what it would be like to have that tongue roving all over your body in a space bigger than the seat of this car. A king-size bed, for instance.

You're about to invite him in, but then you feel something vibrating underneath you. You pull back from the kiss in surprise, and he laughs, holding you more loosely, shifting in his seat to pull out his phone. You put a finger to your lips as he answers it, his mouth so close to your ear you can feel the heat of his breath.

"Hello," he says. "Yes. Yes. Taken care of. I'll be there in twenty." Then he puts the phone away again. "Duty calls. I'm afraid I have to go."

"Do you really? I'm sorry."

"Trust me, I'm sorrier." He takes your face in his hands and kisses you passionately again.

"But I didn't even get to return the favor."

He tugs on your chin and smiles. "It's okay. I kind of like the thought of you owing me one."

"Hey, you know where I live."

He opens the car door and somehow manages to stand, still holding you comfortably in his arms, as if you weigh nothing. Then he effortlessly places you, legs still shaky, on the pavement. He leans in through the window to retrieve your shoes and bag. Then he drops to his knees in front of you. You hold on to his muscular shoulder for balance, your pussy pulsing again at the feel of him, as he gently slips first one shoe and then the other onto your bare feet. Then he stands and kisses you again. At last he pulls away, but as he touches the door handle, he turns back to kiss you one last time.

"I'll watch you in," he says with a nod toward your front door.

"Ever the bodyguard," you say as you turn to walk inside.

"At your service," he says with a smile and a salute. "Night, Ms. Lewis Hamilton."

"Night, Mr. Bodyguard. And thanks again. That was—wow—'fun' is putting it mildly."

Once you're safely inside the building, you turn and watch as the 350Z speeds off into the night. He lifts his arm out of the sunroof and waves.

All you want now is to collapse onto your sofa and unwind, maybe with a DVD and a bowl of popcorn.

❧ Go to *page 238*.

a girl walks into a bar

> ᕫ Miles's box of tricks wasn't your style, so you
>   got out of there

 YOU SETTLE BACK IN the taxi and breathe out. That business with the suitcase full of toys was starting to get a little too kinky for your liking. You're glad you got out of there. There's no denying that Miles is sexy as hell, but if you didn't know it before, you know it now—whips and chains just aren't your style.

As the driver maneuvers through the streets, you smile to yourself at the crazy night you've had so far. There was the weirdo with the chest wig; the crazy, arrogant rock star; his mountainous bodyguard; that gorgeous woman in the ladies' room at the bar—not forgetting the young barman with a body to make a grown woman weep. And that was just the warm-up—no wonder you're feeling so turned on.

You consider swinging past your local late-night coffee shop for a hot chocolate on your way home. Although, the idea of your bed is alluring, but not necessarily for sleep. There's a hungry ache between your legs that needs attending to. It might just be the perfect night to break that Rabbit out of its packaging.

🌚 If you want to swing past your local coffee shop on the way home, go to page 242.

🌚 If you want to go straight home to your Rabbit, go to page 253.

a girl walks into a bar

🪱 You've decided to go back to the bar for one
last drink

🍸 You HEAD INSIDE A little cautiously, but there's no
sign of the rock stars or their groupies—and, more important, Chest Wig—thank goodness. The bar is still a
little busy, but the seat you had much earlier is empty,
and you head for it and sit down with a sigh of relief.
Your shoes are surprisingly comfortable (so they should
be, at that price), but even so, there's only so long a girl
can ramble around in heels this high.

There's a fairly noisy group of women next to you,
having some sort of girls' night out, drinking highly colored cocktails by the bucketful. You spot the adorable
bartender, who has his hands full with them as they
heckle and flirt manically.

He catches your eye, and unless you're completely de-
luded, his face lights up. He mouths, "Be right there,"
and goes back to doling out drinks to a brassy blonde

who's trying to push her business card down the front of his shirt.

It's too noisy to ring Melissa—the woman on the seat next to you is calling for her drink and waving vigorously at the bartender—so you tap out a message to her as he hastens down the bar with a lurid pink concoction in his hand.

With half an eye, you notice as your neighbor snatches the drink from him and shrieks, "Bottoms up!"

The next second, the contents of her glass rain down on you as she slides off the back of her seat and crashes to the ground, arms windmilling.

Her friends screech and rush to her aid, but although she's swearing a blue streak, she seems unhurt. You wish you could say the same for your favorite black dress. Most of her drink—can it really only have been one glass? it feels like a gallon—managed to catch you full on your chest, and you can feel it oozing down your cleavage and dripping onto your lap. There are also splatters all over your face, arms, and neck, as well as your phone and your bag.

You look down at the damage in despair—you look like a contestant in a wet-T-shirt competition, but not in a good way. The drink is clearly sugary, and as it oozes over you, the stickiness feels hideous.

A damp cloth materializes under your nose, held out by the bartender. "I'm so sorry," he says. "I should have refused to serve her—she was completely wasted."

"It's not your fault," you say, noting the total lack of any apology coming your way from the gang of women,

a girl walks into a bar

now noisily heading for the exit. Your drunken assailant, tottering and still cursing, is being supported by her slightly more sober pals. You hope that tomorrow she wakes up with a hangover like an elephant sitting on her head.

You dab at your chest, but it's going to take more than one towel to clean up this mess. You're really annoyed; it's been a weird night as it is, and you're very fond of this dress, which is going to need specialist industrial-strength cleaning after this.

"Is there anything I can do to help?" The barman is hovering anxiously, looking almost as upset as you feel.

"No, but thanks. Wait—maybe you can call a taxi for me? I'm going to have to go home and scrub down."

"At this time of night it'll take at least twenty minutes for a taxi to get here," he says. "Um . . . you could always go upstairs to our place and use our bathroom."

" 'Our place'? Upstairs?"

"Yes, my cousin lives upstairs: the apartment goes with the job. I'm crashing there, looking after the place while I fill in for him. It's completely private. Tiny, but you could, um, wipe yourself down or whatever, and wash out your dress, you know, until we can find you a ride home."

You're tempted. You really want to get this hideous slushy goo off you—the thought of having to wait until you get home is unendurable.

"Please, it's really no trouble. I feel awful," he goes on. "Look, there's my manager. Things have quieted

down a bit. I'm sure he won't mind if I duck out early. He can manage the bar for the last hour or so, so I can help you out."

The manager, alerted by the commotion, is already on the scene, arranging for someone to whisk away the broken glass and mop the floor. Now he leans over toward you and apologizes as well: "We're so sorry about this, ma'am. I'll personally arrange drinks on the house for you and a friend next time you come in."

He exchanges a few words with the bartender, who turns to you, smiling. "It's cool, he'll handle things down here. C'mon, let's get you out of that dress."

A split second later he registers the words he's just spoken and blushes to the tips of his fingers. You've never seen a man go that red before. He's so mortified that, even in your exasperated state, you can't help smiling, and you notice the manager is also suppressing a grin.

"Lead on," you say as cheerfully as you can manage.

You FOLLOW HIM THROUGH an exit behind the bar and into a rather bleak corridor with a featureless black door. This leads to a narrow flight of stairs that takes you up to apartments above the bar. On the second floor, you pass a small room with fluorescent lights, and the bartender points to a row of coin-operated washing machines and driers. "See, we can have your clothes washed and dried in no time."

a girl walks into a bar

He leads you into a tiny and rather chaotic apartment. There's a mountain bike cluttering up the hall, piles of books everywhere, and the world's smallest galley kitchen on the right.

Your new friend gestures to the bathroom on the left. You look in gingerly, but surprisingly for a bachelor pad, it's clean, even if the bathtub is several decades old. There's shaving clutter on the shelves over the sink, and a towel hanging askew off the rack, but you've seen much worse, including in your own bathroom back home.

"Here, let me find you a towel . . . You can shower if you like. There's washing stuff in the cabinet under the sink for your dress, if you need it."

The bartender presses a towel of about the same vintage as the bath into your arms, but it's large and spotlessly clean. Then he retreats. "You take your time. I'll make us something hot to drink in the meantime."

The second the bathroom door closes, you strip off your dress and view the damage. You're going to have to rinse out the entire garment: the slushy liquid has soaked right through. But how are you going to get out of here without clothes? You'll have to borrow a shirt or something.

Your bra is also saturated, and you drag it off as well. Great. Now you're clad in a G-string, heels, and the remains of a large pink cocktail, in a total stranger's student-style bathroom, with not a stitch to wear. And you're still covered in sticky goo.

You strip down completely and step into the bath, where you figure out which nozzles to turn and use the old-fashioned handheld showerhead to rinse the gunk off yourself. You reach for the shower gel, which smells pleasantly of limes. The water is comfortingly hot, and you start to feel marginally better, even though your eye makeup is probably pure panda by now, and your carefully styled hair has gone all fluffy in the steam.

Climbing out, you wash the dress and your bra in the sink, squeeze out as much water as possible, and then blot them with the towel. Now what? You wrap the towel around yourself and knot it firmly above your breasts, then crack open the door cautiously.

"Um, hello? Do you think I can use the drier?" you call. "And do you have a T-shirt or something I can borrow?"

The bartender sticks his head out of the kitchen and does a double take.

"What?" you ask defensively.

"Nothing, you just look younger," he blurts. "Wait, I'll get you a shirt. Hang on . . ."

He dives through another door and emerges again with a vast T-shirt. "Give me your clothes. I'll bring them down to the laundry room." You hand over your wet dress and your bra, and this time you both blush.

He recovers first. "Back in a second. There's chai tea in the kitchen whenever you're ready."

You retreat to the bathroom and investigate your new outfit. The slogan across the front reads:

a girl walks into a bar

God is dead. —*Nietzsche*
Nietzsche is dead. —*God*

Could this evening get any more bizarre? you wonder. You've gone from being a confident, grown-up woman on a night out to a walking debating-society ad—and missing half your underwear. You wriggle back into your G-string and heels, don the T-shirt, and wipe the worst of the mascara-smudge from under your eyes. It's a fairly weird look—the bartender is right. You do look younger with your scrubbed face and slumber-party-queen shirt. The hooker heels cancel out the innocence, though, but you're not sure you want to pad around a strange place in bare feet.

Time to head back to the kitchen. On the fridge, you spot a calendar of shifts for the bar downstairs, and you're intrigued to see the single initial X written into many of the spaces. It reminds you of treasure maps, where X marks the spot.

On cue, the bartender bounces back into the kitchen. "So, your clothes should be dry in about forty-five minutes. I really am so sorry about this. I feel terrible—"

"What does the X stand for here?" you ask, as much to cut off another round of apologies as out of curiosity.

"Oh!" He looks slightly sheepish. "That's me. My name's Xavier—I know, I know, it sounds like a porn star's name, so my family and friends call me X. At least, that's how my cousin marks up the shift rotation. Honey in your chai?"

Helena L. Paige

Honey in your chai? You suppress a giggle. What sort of student *is* he?

"Um, I think so," you say. He pours a fragrant caramel-colored liquid into two mugs and arranges them on a tray with honey and spoons. "Follow me," he says, picking up the tray and heading down the short hallway, pushing a door open with his shoulder.

It's clearly his bedroom, and you hesitate in the doorway, but he's already apologizing: "I'm so sorry, we don't have a living room—my cousin turned it into his crash pad. We could hang out in the kitchen . . . ?"

"No, this is cool," you say. In fact, you're fascinated. You were expecting smelly sneakers and game consoles, but it's a cross between a monk's cell and some mysterious Eastern grotto. The three-quarter bed has a plain white cover, and there's a Japanese print on the wall. There are candles everywhere and incense burning on the window ledge. There's also a little bronze Buddha on the bedside table, a rolled-up yoga mat in the corner, and books everywhere—piled up next to the bed, in the towers of wine crates he's using as shelves, and on the old-fashioned desk, where a silver laptop has pride of place.

You love it when there are books in a room—it makes it much easier to start a conversation, plus you can tell so much about somebody by looking at their books. You wander over to browse and immediately spot the kind of things you'd expect for someone interested in Eastern religions—masses of titles about Hinduism, tai chi,

a girl walks into a bar

Persian poetry, and all that sort of thing, but also a lot of speculative fiction. You don't know much about it, but you recognize the good stuff—David Mitchell's *Cloud Atlas*, Margaret Atwood's *The Handmaid's Tale*, plenty of Ursula K. Le Guin and Philip Pullman.

"I loved this," you say, tugging at *Cloud Atlas*. "Have you seen the movie?" You pull a little harder to release the book, and the one next to it comes loose and tumbles to the floor. "Oops, sorry," you say, bending to retrieve it. It isn't until you straighten and catch sight of Xavier's face, which is crimson again, his mouth hanging slightly open, that you remember that you're wearing a T-shirt that falls as far as your thighs and is doing a fair job of keeping you decent—as long as you don't bend over.

You sit down hastily on the bed, tugging the shirt down as far as it will go. To break the charged moment, you sip your drink, which smells peppery and perfumed at the same time—and almost choke.

"Do you like it?" Xavier asks eagerly. "Or did I put in too much chili?"

"You put chili in *tea*?" you ask as the flames on your tongue die down.

He launches into an enthusiastic list of the spices he uses to make it from scratch, and how he learned to make it properly while traveling in India during his last backpacking trip.

Once he's run out of chai recipes, there's another long silence—not awkward, exactly, but fizzing, rather. At last Xavier blurts out, "I'm sorry, I'm not exactly used to having women in my room."

Helena S. Paige

You laugh. "Are you kidding me? Every time I looked your way tonight, someone was hitting on you. You probably have a different gorgeous woman up here every other night. I'm surprised there aren't grooves in the stairs!"

He locks his hands, and looks down at them. "Um, no. You're the first."

"Wait, you're not saying—I mean, you must have a string of girlfriends, looking the way you do . . ."

He shakes his head.

"But how is it possible . . . ?"

"Oh, I dunno. Only child. Older parents. They're cool, but they were really strict. Quaker boarding school. First year of university in a seminary . . ."

"What? You were studying to be a priest?"

"No, no. It was a place to crash—one of my lecturers knew I was looking for something cheap and quiet. It was great while I found my feet, but it wasn't exactly the sort of place I could bring friends. And when I moved on, everyone else had sort of hooked up, and I never knew how to get into the swing of all that stuff."

As the full implications of what he's saying slowly dawn on you, you can't believe you're about to ask such an intimate question—but then you're the one dressed in almost nothing but a borrowed T-shirt. "Xavier, are you saying you're . . . a virgin?"

This time he doesn't blush. He goes very still. And then he nods.

"Um, wow." You need a minute to process this. The guy looks like sex on legs. It seems impossible that some woman hasn't gobbled him up.

a girl walks into a bar

He hurries on: "I know, I must seem like a freak to you, but you saw tonight how women act around me. They all assume I've been around the block hundreds of times. How could I get one of them up here and then say, 'Um, actually I'm a virgin and I haven't the first clue where to start'? They'd laugh in my face."

You winch your jaw back up and wonder how to handle things from here. Xavier looks like he fell off the roof of a cathedral, but you came out for a night of fun, not to play Dr. Ruth. Still, you're tempted to take him in hand, as it were. He has the most mouthwatering body you've seen in a long time, after all . . . You tell yourself it would be an act of kindness to offer. Plus you never know, you might even have fun.

On the other hand, it's not something to be taken lightly. Your first time wasn't earth-shattering, but you'll always remember it *because* it was the first time. Do you want to take on that kind of responsibility?

❧ If this isn't for you, and you decide to hotfoot it out of there, go to page 197.

❧ If you decide to stick around and show him a thing or two, go to page 200.

Helena S. Paige

🐍 You've decided this isn't for you

You LOOK INTO HIS eager eyes. He's gorgeous and there's definitely chemistry in the air, but it's been a long night, and it's too late to play schoolteacher.

And he really is very young. He's about the same age as the sweet but slightly naïve student intern you're mentoring at work. Wait a minute; they'd be perfect for each other! They like the same kinds of books, they both want to travel, and while you're not sure if Lexi is a virgin or not, she has that whole sunny, innocent thing going on—and she's definitely single. Why not let them fumble around together, having fun working out where and how their body parts are supposed to fit? You feel a quick pang of envy for all the discovery ahead of them, but you shake it off. There's plenty of fun to be had out in Adultland.

"You know . . ." you say. "I might have a solution to your, ah, problem. I think I know the perfect girl for you."

"You do?" he says, his eyes shining.

"We have this intern at work, Lexi—she just turned twenty. I think you two might hit it off."

"Really?"

"Absolutely. She's gorgeous, funny, and clever. And she's into yoga and meditation, that sort of thing. I think you might be just right for each other."

Xavier tears a page out of a notebook on his desk, writes a number on it, then hands it to you. "Cool. Maybe she can give me a call sometime?" he says. "And thanks. I really appreciate it."

"At the risk of sounding like your older sister, can I give you some advice? Try not to stress about the whole thing. Just ask a woman out. Kiss her. See where that takes you."

"Thanks again." Xavier gets to his feet and ambles over to you. Then he leans down and kisses you softly on the cheek. His lips are soft and warm, and his breath fans against your skin. There's a long quiet moment, and then he turns his head very tentatively and lays his mouth against yours. It's so gentle, it's hardly a kiss, just a long, slow brush of that heavenly mouth. It takes everything you have not to respond. If Lexi plays her cards right, she's going to be one lucky girl.

One of the candles sputters and the moment is broken. You have a life to get back to.

"Do you think my dress will be dry yet?" you ask. "It's late. I think I'm going to head out."

Helena L. Paige

"Yeah, absolutely, we can go past the laundry room on your way out," he says, leading you to the door. "It's been really nice meeting you. Again, I'm sorry about the drink and the dress."

"That's okay. Everything happens for a reason. And I've got a funny feeling Lexi might just be the reason in this case."

You smile at each other, and you feel that tug at your heart again. You hope he finds what he's looking for. Meanwhile, it's time you called it a night and went home. Or maybe you should perk yourself up with something from your local coffee shop en route?

❧ If you go straight home, go to page 217.

❧ If you go home via your local late-night coffee shop, go to page 242.

a girl walks into a bar

❧ You've decided to stick around and show him a
thing or two

 You DECIDE TO TAKE the plunge: "Xavier, would
you like me to change all of that?"

Your words hang in the air between you, and you
add, "If you've never had sex before, at least I could show
you where to start."

He looks at you with a mix of disbelief, caution, and
wild hope. "Would you?"

"I would. But here are the ground rules: There are no
strings. This is a one-off. You've been really sweet to me,
you're one of the hottest guys I've ever seen, and all I want
is to give you a lovely, unpressured first time. No need to
romance me or worry about performance or any of that
stuff. Okay? Just relax, go with it, have a good time."

Then a thought strikes you. "You do have condoms,
don't you?"

Oops. From the consternation on his face, this is not an

eventuality he has covered. And while you keep meaning to be a grown-up and stash an emergency condom in your bag, it hasn't been a priority—until now.

His look of agony is almost funny, but you're also frustrated. It looks like you're going to have to revise your offer, but then his face clears. "Wait, hang on! Don't move! Stay right there!" He shoots out of the room in almost comical haste.

A minute later he's back, panting proudly and carrying—what is that, a *gross* of condoms? There must be hundreds in the cardboard box he's brought in. Now that's optimism for you.

"My cousin keeps the stocks for refilling the dispensers in the bathrooms in the bar," Xavier grins. "Lucky I remembered."

You're just relieved to have the problem solved.

"So we're on? Just this one time, no strings?"

He smiles at you again, and it's that same stomach-melting smile he gave you when you first walked into the bar. "Okay, it's a deal. But are you sure? I mean—"

"Xavier," you say. "Stop talking." You go over to him, and let yourself slowly down onto his lap. His arms come round you, and you feel the warmth of his body and the thudding of his heart. You sink your head onto his shoulder and place your fingers on the exquisite little hollow at the base of his throat, which is pulsing in time with his heartbeat. You rest like that for a moment, and then you go searching for his mouth.

It tastes of spice and tea, and his lips are incredibly soft. At first he is tentative, then more eager, murmuring

a girl walks into a bar

as your tongues touch, probing into each other's mouths. He reaches up to cradle your cheek, changing the angle of your head, deepening the kiss, growing more confident. When you finally break for air, you're both breathing fast and smiling.

"So far, so good," you say. "Let's go a little farther, shall we?"

In the soft light of his desk lamp, you're touched to see his hands trembling slightly. They're beautiful, the hands of a concert pianist, with fingers that manage to be delicate and strong at the same time. You pick one up, press a kiss into the hollow, then place it over one of your breasts.

The result is instantaneous: you both gasp with pleasure as your nipple pops up against his palm through the thin fabric of the T-shirt. He kneads and cups gently at first, then more robustly as you press your breast against his hand. Then his fingers seek out and play with your nipple, tweaking at it with gentle, teasing pinches.

You whimper, and his hand stills immediately. "Too much?"

"God, no. Trust me, I'll tell you if anything is too much. But I think it's time to return the favor."

Part of you has been wanting to undress him since you first saw him behind the bar, and you take your time, first unbuttoning his shirt, then slowly raising it over his perfect stomach and his chest, which is smooth and hairless. He lifts his arms above his head as you peel it all the way off and drop it on the floor at your feet, revealing his perfection. In the candlelight, his torso glows, and his skin is as fine as cashmere over muscles that ripple as your hand glides over them. You suck your index finger and then stroke it over each nipple in turn, and he shudders. When you follow up with your mouth, he groans aloud.

You're torn between wanting to draw out this languid stage of your seduction, and the urgent beating between your legs. You're definitely both still wearing too many clothes, and so you get up from his lap, causing Xavier to protest—until you pull your own T-shirt languorously off over your head.

"I think it's time to get over to the bed," you say.

"Wait," he says hoarsely. "I just want to look at you for a minute—in that tiny lace thing—and those heels . . . You have no idea how hot you look."

You stand in front of him, reveling in the effect you're having. You part your legs and sway a little, stretching your arms up over your head and arching your back slightly, making your breasts rise and bob.

"I'm all yours. Look all you want."

In seconds he's up off his chair, fumbling at the button of his jeans. You hear the sound of his zipper as he yanks it down in a hurry, then he's hopping from foot to foot as he strips his pants off. His body, as it emerges, is more amazing than you could have hoped—narrow hips, taut belly, legs that go on forever, and a tight, high butt, now clad only in thin cotton shorts. Which do nothing to hide the size of his erection.

"I think we need to get totally naked," you tell him. You step out of your G-string, then sit primly on the

a girl walks into a bar

edge of the bed, knees together as you kick off your shoes. Then, slowly and deliberately, you lean back on your arms, open your legs, and tilt your pelvis up toward him. You've never been this wanton before, but then you can't remember when you were last this wet.

You drop a hand between your legs and stroke your swollen lips apart, your fingers making soft sucking sounds on your wet, heated flesh.

Xavier's eyes dilate and he murmurs something under his breath as he wrenches off his shorts. It's your turn to stare as his cock springs free, fully erect, long and thick, the head shining with moisture.

"Lie down." You have to clear your throat to get the words out as you pat the bed next to you.

He whispers, "This is, like, unreal. I can't believe it's happening. You're incredible." Then the bed sags as he lies down beside you.

You look at his body trembling with need and pent-up lust. You should take this slowly, but you're not sure if either of you can at this stage. And you can't resist his cock, which is dusky and engorged. You wrap a hand around it, the silky skin taut over the live rock underneath, and squeeze, then pull your hand just once from the base of it up to the tip—and with a great shout he convulses, shooting hot semen into the air in huge spurts.

Dammit, you should have seen that coming—pun intended. What's the protocol for a situation like this? you wonder, trying not to feel disappointed. Once

Xavier has his breath and his voice back, he starts apologizing—again.

"Shhh," you say, reaching for the borrowed T-shirt to blot at the come pooling on his flat belly, still heaving. "That was inevitable. I should have, um, handled things more carefully."

"I'll completely understand if you want to leave," he pants.

❧ If you decide it's time to leave, go to page 206.

❧ If you want to stick around for lesson number two, go to page 209.

a girl walks into a bar

🐍 You've decided to leave

 YOU LEAN UP ON one elbow and look at him. It's hardly a surprise that it all happened so quickly—after all, he's been waiting for this moment for years. You sigh as you watch his eyelids fluttering, his chest still visibly rising and falling.

You could always just head home. You picture the box in the drawer next to your bedside table, and the vibrator nestled in it. You remember what your girlfriends say about vibrators: they never come before you, there's no awkward small talk, they don't hog the remote control, and you don't ever have to wonder if they'll call.

You lean down and kiss Xavier gently on the lips, stroking his fringe out of his face.

"You're delicious, you know that?" you say, smiling into his eyes.

He grins back ruefully. "Sorry that was so quick," he says. "We didn't even get to . . . you know . . ."

"That's okay," you say. "That was just lesson number one. When you're ready for lesson number two, you grab one of those dozens of girls panting at your feet and whip them up to this room, okay?"

He nods, his face still drowsy with satisfaction.

"It's late. I need to get out of here," you say, slipping off the side of the bed and reaching for the shirt he was wearing.

"Are you sure?" he asks, propping himself up on his elbows, looking a little disappointed. "If you give me five minutes I'm sure I can, you know . . . get things going again."

You lean forward and press a hand down firmly on his shoulder. "You know what? It's really late, and you look like you need your beauty sleep. I'm exhausted, too." He lies back and watches you with dreamy eyes as you slip his cotton shirt on over your head, breathing in the boy scent of him, then step back into your G-string.

"You don't mind, do you?" you say, tugging his shirt into place, "I'm just going to grab my dress on the way out. I can leave your shirt for you in the laundry room, if that's okay."

"Why don't you keep it, and bring it back tomorrow night?" he says, that extraordinary smile lighting up his face again. "For our second lesson."

You consider him thoughtfully. "I might just do that."

"I get off at midnight," he says. "And then again at one, two, three, and four."

You laugh and blow him a quick kiss as you grab your bag and shoes and slip out the door.

a girl walks into a bar

Next stop is the laundry room, where the drier has just come to a stop. You pull out your dress and bra and slip into them. They're warm and fresh. You take one last sniff of the bartender's shirt and smile: Who would have thought you'd find a virgin in this day and age, especially one with the looks of an angel? It's the equivalent of finding a unicorn. You fold his shirt up and leave it on top of the drier, acknowledging a little wistfully that you're unlikely to be coming back. Now you need something to perk you up. Perhaps a hot chocolate on your way home? Or maybe that Rabbit in your bedside drawer will do the trick . . .

❧ If you're not quite ready to go home yet, go to page 240.

❧ If you decide to swing past your local late-night coffee shop on your way home, go to page 242.

❧ If you decide to go home to your Rabbit, go to page 253.

❧ You're sticking around for lesson number two

"I'M NOT GOING ANYWHERE," you say. Especially not with your body nagging for its own release. You have definitely not finished with Xavier. In fact, you've barely begun.

You cuddle into him as his breathing slowly returns to normal, kissing his cheek and his soft hair, which smells faintly of the lime shower gel in the bathroom, and something more human and warm as well.

"I want to make it up to you," he whispers. "How about a back massage?"

That's not a bad idea at all. Your body is knotted with tension, and your lower back aches faintly, no doubt as a result of wandering around all evening in five-inch heels. You're willing to give it a go, and you roll over. You feel the bed move as he gets up, and a minute later you hear him rubbing oil between his hands, a faint scent of sandalwood in the air.

Next, his hands come down on your shoulders, the oil slightly heated, and you sigh luxuriously. His fingers press skillfully into your tense muscles, running over the knots but not digging in, smoothing and warming the flesh.

"Wow," you mumble against the pillow. "You really know what you're doing."

"I did a course at the ashram in India," he says.

That makes sense—he's not slapping your muscles around or pinching at the knots. Rather it feels as if he's drawing connections between the muscle and nerve groups of your back, calming them, deeply relaxing them. You fall into a trance where all that exists are his warm, strong, stroking fingers circling slowly all the way down your spine. You're almost on the brink of sleep when his touch changes, becoming lighter. He draws his fingertips across the skin of your back, and you shiver at the shift in pressure, goose bumps rising. He draws a path of gooseflesh right down to the base of your spine, then circles his hands very lightly on your buttocks, teasing as much as soothing. His hands go lower and lower, and by now you're holding your breath.

You're also becoming aware that it's not just his hands that are nudging your bottom—as he straddles you, you become aware of the hot, hard pressure of his unfurling and rising cock against you, and the pulse between your legs becomes urgent once more.

Helena L. Paige

"Xavier," you murmur, "I think you've missed a spot." He gets the message right away, clambering off you and helping you roll onto your back, which feels brand-new.

You stretch and press your chest upward, and he gets the hint, trailing a hand over your breasts. You wriggle, tucking your arms behind your head to give him free access. He moves his head down and you gasp as his mouth closes around the tip of one breast, drawing in skin, areola, and nipple, tongue fluttering.

God, the guy is a natural at this; you'd never have thought he was a novice. His hair trails across your breasts as he alternates between sucking and licking, and starting to nip very gently as he gets bolder. The feel of his teeth against your rock-hard nipples has your hips lifting off the bed. Jeez, you've heard of women coming just from having their breasts caressed, and you're beginning to understand that it's a real possibility.

You're growing frantic, and you capture his hand, drawing it down between your thighs. You hook one leg across him, so that his fingers have full access, and guide his index finger to your clit. Seconds later, you cry out as he presses down on the supersensitive little pearl of flesh, and then his eager fingers slide down, exploring further.

"You're so wet," he murmurs, "I feel like I've found the source of the Nile," and even though you're practically writhing with pleasure, you laugh. And then moan out loud as one cool, long finger slides in and up, slowly, all the way.

a girl walks into a bar

"How does that feel?" he whispers, pressing first one finger, then two, into your soaking pussy. "It feels fantastic to me."

"Delirious," you mutter, thrashing now, eager to come. You can feel his penis pressing hard against your hip, and your good intentions to get on top of him and make the sex last as long as possible are swept aside.

You seize his cock again, and it's satisfyingly hard and hot. "I want you to come inside me," you say.

His eyes and his teeth gleam at that, and then he flails at the box next to the bed and scoops up a whole handful of condoms. Even though you're both ferociously aroused, you giggle like teenagers.

"I think you only need one of those at a time," you say.

As it's his first time, you deal with the condom, getting it out of the packet, pinching it at the top and carefully unrolling it down the length of his shaft. Then you tug him over on top of you, open your legs wider, and pull up your knees, settling him between your legs.

You can feel his cock nudging eagerly at you, and you're equally keen for him to come inside you, but you need to get this right.

You reach your head up and kiss him, sweeping your hands down his back, all the way to his tight buttocks. Then you tilt your groin up against his at the same time as tugging gently at his bottom and, to your enormous relief, he slides his cock into you easily, naturally, the angle perfect, the sensation an overwhelming rush of pleasure.

Helena L. Paige

You both groan deeply at the feel of him stretching the wet, warm, tender skin of your cunt, and you give him a tiny squeeze. He groans again.

Then he smiles down at you. "I cannot tell you how good this feels. It was so worth the wait. Are you okay?"

"More than okay," you sigh. "Please just fuck me now. Nice and slow. And hard."

And he does, each stroke a burn of pleasure that goes deeper and deeper. It doesn't take long—you can feel your orgasm building, and you pray he holds on long enough, and then it blasts through your body, the relief of it so strong it brings tears to your eyes. You're dimly aware of screaming softly as you arch over and over again, grabbing on to his shoulders like a raft as the world spins around, and then it's his turn, and he shudders rackingly, pouring his orgasm into you, shouting in triumph.

Then the only sound is your ragged breathing as you lie limp and glued together, your heart banging against your rib cage, his head buried in your neck. Your limbs are boneless, but you're just able to stroke the back of Xavier's neck and shoulders, feeling the fine mist of sweat that's sprung out all over his body.

You can feel his cock slowly shrinking inside you, the afterglow intense as you clasp him in your still-swollen pussy. He slips out, holding the condom in place, and you both sigh. It takes an aeon before you return to anything like normal consciousness. At last he begins to feel heavy, and you gently press at his shoulders.

a girl walks into a bar

Xavier gets the hint immediately and slides off you, clasping you loosely in his arms as you cuddle for the second time. His voice is full of sleepy pride: "Wow. That was . . . just wow." And then a sudden anxious note: "You did enjoy that, didn't you? I thought you did, it certainly sounded like it. And it felt incredible when you came like that—I mean, I assumed, you did come, didn't you?"

"No, you idiot, I was having an unexpected epileptic fit crossed with the hiccups. Of course that was an orgasm, and I loved it. You were amazing."

You giggle quietly together, then doze for a few minutes. The sense of warm honey flooding all your veins is irresistible, but there's a tiny voice in your head prodding you to get up and go home. If you stay the night, things are going to get complicated.

"Xavier," you say. "Wake up. I hate to break up this party, but I need to go home."

He protests, groggily, but you're firm. "Remember what we said, this is just a one-off."

He clasps your hand and tugs it to his lips. "But I want to do this again. And again and again and again. And then some more. And then about another hundred times. And then I'd like to start all over again."

You're both moved and flattered. And so very tempted. He looks like a fallen angel, lying on the bed, his cock now quiet on his flawless thigh, his eyes sleepy. Get a grip, you scold yourself.

He kisses your hand again and you weaken for a

moment. And then you remind yourself, he's a student. With all the angst of growing up still ahead, and loads and loads of student girls, with their issues and dramas and their soul-searching. Not to mention their perfect nineteen-year-old bodies. Xavier is the type to fall in love and break hearts and get his heart broken, and it all still lies ahead for him. He needs to get on with doing all that, and you need to get on with your life.

You get up slowly and retrieve your underwear and shoes. Then you lean over, kissing him lingeringly one last time.

"Goodbye, Xavier. You're going to make some lucky woman—or maybe quite a few lucky women—very happy, you know."

"I'll never forget you," he whispers earnestly. "Not if I live to be ninety and have sex with millions more women."

"It was my pleasure. Literally. Now go back to sleep. I'm going to call a taxi. I'll wait for it downstairs in the bar."

He doesn't fight you anymore. He turns onto his side with a contented sigh, and his impossibly long lashes flutter down onto his impossibly perfect cheeks. His last words, almost on the verge of sleep: "Well, you know where to find me, if you want me."

You're done for the night. All you want is your own bed. But this last adventure has been so sweet and un-

a girl walks into a bar

expected, you're tempted to drop in on Melissa and tell her the whole story.

❦ If you go straight home, go to page 217.

❦ If you want to drop by Melissa's to tell her about your night, go to page 249.

Helena d. Paige

216

❧ You've decided to call it a night; it's time to go home

It's late. In fact, it's so late it's almost early. Your night out has been a lot of fun and quite the adventure, but you're thankful to be heading home at last. Even though you're exhausted, adrenaline is still spiking through your body. Sleep feels very far away, but that's okay. You don't have any plans for tomorrow and you've got *Bridget Jones's Diary* on DVD, which you've been wanting to watch again for ages. That movie never gets old.

You're not used to wearing such insanely high heels anymore. Your feet are aching, and your purple G-string, as fabulous as it is, might just be strangling you from the bottom up. It's going to be bliss to stop sucking in your tummy, pull on your comfy pants, and climb onto the couch with a cup of tea, a bowl of popcorn, and the remote control.

All's quiet as you step into the lobby of your apartment building. You press the elevator button and glance up at the row of numbers above the door. According to the little light, the elevator is stuck on the sixth floor. That's your floor.

You press the button again a couple of times, and then shake your head—why do people do that? It's not as if it ever makes the elevator arrive any faster. When you look up again, the light is still glowing on the sixth floor. You're annoyed. Which idiot neighbor is holding up the elevator at this time of night?

You look to your left—there's always the stairs.

☘ If you decide to take the stairs, go to page 219.

☘ If you decide to wait for the elevator—your
     feet are killing you—go to page 234.

Helena L. Paige

❧ You've decided to take the stairs

By the time you're halfway up the stairs, you have to stop, bending at the waist and panting. What possessed you to pick the stairs, especially in these heels? Who tries to be a hero at 4 a.m.?

When you finally make it to the sixth floor, you push open the stairwell door. You're dying to get home and get your shoes off, so you hurry forward in the dim light. The next second, you're yelping as you skin your shins on something unmoving. You instinctively stretch out both arms to brace yourself as you come crashing down.

"Fuck!" You look to see what you tripped over, and discover it's one of about twenty cardboard boxes scattered randomly along the passage. What kind of moron would leave all these boxes lying around? Your shins throb and your palms and wrists sting from breaking your fall on the rough carpet. You could have broken your neck!

"Oh my god, are you all right?"

Still on all fours, tears stinging, you twist around to see who's asking.

There's a tall guy in a pair of torn and faded blue jeans, a checked shirt, and glasses standing in the doorway of apartment 610. You've never seen him before—he must be moving in, which explains all the boxes and the jammed elevator. He hurries over and drops to his knees beside you.

"Are you okay? Is anything broken?" He reaches for your elbow and helps you to your feet. Once you're upright, you push the hair from your face and then bend down to rub your shins and evaluate the damage. A big, angry bruise is forming on your left shin.

"Oh no," he says, "you're bleeding! This is all my fault. I'm so sorry! Please come inside. I haven't unpacked the bathroom boxes yet, but I'm sure the one with the bandages is in the kitchen. We need to get you patched up."

☙ If you go into his apartment to stop the bleeding, go to page 221.

☙ If you just want to hobble home, go to page 233.

Helena L. Paige

❧ You've gone into his apartment to stop the bleeding

🍸 YOUR NEW NEIGHBOR TAKES your arm and helps
you limp into his apartment. The layout is almost iden-
tical to yours, but the decor is vastly different. This is
clearly a man's domain. Very few boxes seem to have
been unpacked, and the bulk of them are stacked all over
the place, but the big-screen TV, entertainment system,
and couches are set up as if they've been here forever.

"When did you move in?" you ask.

"A few days ago," he says as he helps you into the
kitchen. "But those boxes in the hall only got dropped off
earlier this evening, and I didn't think anyone would be
around so late, so I thought I could leave them there for
the night. But I really should have stacked them against
the wall. Again, I'm really sorry!"

You can't help smiling a little at how devastated he

looks. "You'll be hearing from my lawyers," you say sternly.

He looks startled, but when he sees you're joking, he grins, and you're taken aback at how good-looking he is. You hadn't noticed it at first. He's definitely not hot in a conventional way, but he has a slightly skewed smile, and the longest eyelashes you've ever seen on a guy— they just about swipe the lenses of his black-framed glasses every time he blinks.

"Do you think you'll be able to hop up here?" he asks, patting the kitchen counter. "Then I can take a closer look at that cut. It's still bleeding, and we should probably clean it."

You lever yourself up onto the counter while he dives into a box on the kitchen table, and then comes toward you, unzipping a small first-aid kit.

"Are you a doctor or something?" you ask, feeling a little queasy at the sight of the blood trickling down your leg.

"Nope, I'm a writer, which is almost the same thing. I mean, I've written about doctors."

"Oh, well, in that case . . ."

"So, let's take a look at what kind of lawsuit I'm facing here," he says, dabbing at your shin with a cotton ball. "Manslaughter, or simply attack with a deadly cardboard box. But I think you should know that I've written about lawyers as well, so you're in for a bit of a battle should this ever get as far as a courtroom."

Aha. He's cute *and* funny. Those are the dangerous ones.

"I'll be fine. The bleeding's almost stopped," you say, taking the cotton ball from him and pressing it against your skin. "It's late. I'd better get home."

"No way!" he says. "You've lost a lot of blood, and I'm responsible. At least let me make you a cup of tea or a drink before you go."

You look at him, hesitating.

"You really can't go yet," he continues. "I haven't even used half the stuff I've got in here." He indicates the rest of the contents of the first-aid kit laying open on the counter. "What's the point of an impressive first-aid kit if you never get to use it? See, there's still Mercurochrome and antiseptic and bandages to go through before I can officially release you. Doctor-writer's orders!"

"Okay," you relent, and he reaches for another cotton ball. Then he holds the back of your calf in one hand while dabbing your shin carefully with the other. Your leg tingles at his touch. You can't believe how gentle he is, this big, barefoot guy. You take a closer look at him. He must be at least six foot, unshaven, with thick, dark, disheveled hair that could do with a trim.

"What's in all those boxes anyway?" you ask. "It was like running into a brick wall."

"It's books," he says, a little bashful. "I have a slight problem: I can't seem to walk past a book without buying it. It's an occupational hazard. That's one of the reasons I had to move—not enough space for books in my last place. Plus, I'd run out of neighbors to trip up."

The bleeding seems to have stopped, and he releases

a girl walks into a bar

your leg and stands up straight. With you sitting on the kitchen counter, his face is almost level with yours. He's close enough that your skin heats, and, unless you're mistaken, his face flushes a little, too, before he busies himself with a bottle of antiseptic and another cotton ball.

"This may sting a little bit," he says earnestly. "Just squeeze my shoulder if you need to."

That's silly, you think, how sore can it— "Ouch, that stings!" you yell, grabbing hold of his shoulder, feeling his muscles ripple under your hand. The pain is gone as quickly as it came, and you let go of his shoulder reluctantly, feeling silly for making such a fuss. He reaches for a Band-Aid, tears off its wrapper, and covers the gash on your shin, wiping it down gently. And for a brief moment you wonder if he's going to kiss your leg better—the thought of it sends a little thrill up your spine—but he doesn't.

"In my unprofessional opinion, the other leg looks okay—the bruising should go down in a couple of days. I don't have any arnica, but I hear that's good for bruises. Once again, I can't tell you how sorry I am. What's your boyfriend going to say when you come hobbling home all cut and bruised?"

"I don't have a boyfriend," you say. "What about you?"

"I don't have a boyfriend, either," he says, that lopsided smile breaking across his face. You laugh and climb off the counter.

"Can I at least prescribe something for the pain

before you go?" He opens his fridge and peers inside. "My shift at the hospital just ended, and I think I need a drink myself."

If you needed any confirmation of his single status, it's right there on the shelves. The only items in there are a couple of six-packs, a quart of milk, and some Chinese-takeout cartons.

He takes out a beer, twists off the top, and offers it to you.

❧ If you have a drink with him, go to page 226.

❧ If you decide to call it a night, go to page 231.

a girl walks into a bar

❧ You've decided to have a drink with the neighbor

You ACCEPT THE BEER and thank him. The bottle is refreshingly cool, and you can't resist holding it to your cheeks, which still seem to be burning. He grabs another beer for himself and clinks the neck of his bottle against yours.

"To new neighbors," he says.

"And lucrative lawsuits."

You catch his eye, and some kind of current flickers between you.

You follow him into the living room. There are piles of books leaning against just about every wall. You peek into the master bedroom, taking in the unmade king-size bed, strewn with newspapers. An image of the two of you sitting up in bed, drinking coffee and reading the morning paper together, jumps into your mind. You shake off the ridiculous fantasy and sip the ice-cold beer.

"Make yourself comfortable," he says.

You sit on the couch, wondering which chair he'll choose. He sinks into the armchair instead of taking the spot next to you, and you can't help feeling slightly disappointed. You were enjoying having him standing so close to you in the kitchen. There's a manuscript laying on the coffee table, and you pick it up and read the title out loud: *"A Girl Walks into a Bar."*

🖎 If you begin to read the manuscript, go to page 1.

🖎 If you resist the temptation to read his private stuff, go to page 228.

✤ You resist the temptation to read his private stuff

🍹 HE BLUSHES AND TUGS the manuscript out of your hands, dropping it on the floor. "That's just something I'm busy working on. It's still fairly rough."

"Does it have a happy ending?" you ask.

"I don't know yet, but the way things are going, it might have more than one happy ending."

You sit in comfortable silence for a few seconds.

"So did you have a fun night out?" he asks.

You nod and sip your beer. "I really did. I was supposed to meet a friend, but she stood me up at the last minute. But it worked out okay in the end."

"It must have," he says, looking at his watch.

"You can talk. I'm not the only night owl. What on earth are you still doing up?" you ask, looking around, noticing that the TV's off and there's no music playing.

"Working. I like writing at night. It's quiet, and the world has a different feeling when it's late. It's as if anything could happen."

You nod. If only he knew how true that was. You take a last sip of beer. "Speaking of late, I'd better get going," you say.

He stands up with you, looking a little disappointed. "Oh, okay. But maybe you could show me around the area sometime, or we could get a bite to eat? It's the least you can do after bashing into my books like that."

You laugh. "Sure, that sounds like a plan."

"Shall I walk you out? One of the characters in my first novel was a ninja, so I've got the skills to get you home safely. Kind of, anyway. It was never published."

You laugh again. "Ha, I think I should be able to manage all twenty yards. But thanks for the beer, the medical attention, and the scar. I've always wanted a war wound."

"I think I'll probably move those boxes now, to avoid further lawsuits, and also just in case you need to find your way back here at any point. So there won't be any more unfortunate incidents."

You're still giggling as he follows you out the door. You thread your way carefully between boxes as you head toward your own apartment. You can feel his eyes on your back, and you try to look as undisheveled and composed as possible.

At your front door at the other end of the hall, you turn and see that he's still watching you from his door-

a girl walks into a bar

way. He has both hands in his pockets, and that sexy crooked smile on his face.

"Good night," you call softly before letting yourself in.

"Sweet dreams," he calls back with a little wave.

Finally. You're home.

 Go to page 238.

❧ You've decided to call it a night

 "Do you mind if I take a rain check? It's been a very long night."

"Absolutely. How about tomorrow night? I'll need to change your dressing and take a look at that cut," he says, pointing at your shin. "Then maybe dinner? It's the least I can do to make up for causing you such grievous bodily harm. Also, I need someone to show me around my new neighborhood."

You nod. You feel like a duck on the water: calm on the surface but every organ paddling madly on the inside. Surely you're not imagining the chemistry between you. You smooth your dress as you walk to the door with as much composure as you can muster considering the night you've had.

"How's seven o'clock?" he asks.

"Good," you say, stepping around the boxes carefully

and making your way down the passage to your apartment. You can feel his eyes on your back as you go. As you unlock your front door, you look back, and he's leaning against the side of his doorway, his hands in his jeans pockets, that crooked smile perfectly placed. As you go inside, he lifts one hand in a small wave.

❧ To finally go home, go to page 238.

To finally go home, go to page 238.

Helena L. Paige

232

 You just want to hobble home

 "Thank you, that's very kind of you, but it's nothing—it's just a little cut," you say, dabbing at your leg with a tissue. "I'll be fine." You're embarrassed at having tripped in front of him.

"All right," he says. "I'm just glad you're okay."

You walk to your apartment at the end of the hall, trying to look graceful. When you've finally found your keys and unlocked your door, you take a quick look backward and see him busy shifting the boxes from the middle of the hall, piling them up against the walls instead. He looks up at you and waves, smiling a crooked, sexy smile. You wonder if he's single, by any chance.

 To finally go home, go to page 238.

❧ You decided to wait for the elevator; your feet are killing you

WHILE YOU'RE WAITING FOR the elevator, you raise and flex your foot. Your arches are killing you—you can't wait to get these heels off. At last the little red light on the row of floor numbers shifts, and the elevator heads down to pick you up. It's really time to call it a night.

The elevator dings open and you prepare to give whoever was holding it a dirty look, but it's empty.

When you step out of the elevator on the sixth floor, there are piles of cardboard boxes scattered outside apartment 610. Someone must have just moved in; those boxes definitely weren't there when you went out earlier. You crane your neck to see if the door is open, but there are so many boxes piled up in front of it, you can't be sure.

- If you decide to try to catch a glimpse of your new neighbor, go to page 236.

- If your comfy pants and the movie are calling, go to page 238.

a girl walks into a bar

ॐ You've decided to see if you can catch a glimpse
of the new neighbor

YOU CREEP DOWN THE hall toward number 610,
weaving around the boxes dumped randomly along the
way. As you get closer, you see the front door is open and
the lights are on inside. It's almost four in the morning—
who on earth could possibly still be awake at this hour?
Suddenly you hear a man clearing his throat, followed
by the sound of footsteps. Whoever's inside is walking
toward the hallway. He must be coming to fetch one of
the boxes. What will he think if he finds you creeping
around outside his apartment in the middle of the night?

You start speed-walking toward your front door,
hoping that by the time he emerges it will look like you're
casually heading past on your way from the elevator. But
you only make it a couple of steps before you feel a sharp
pain against your shins as you hit something, and then
nose-dive through the air in slow motion. "Fuuuuck!"

you yell, instinctively stretching your arms out to brace yourself as you come crashing down on the ground.

"Ow, ow, ow!" you yell, sprawled unglamorously on the floor with your ass in the air.

"Oh god!" you hear a man's voice behind you.

Mortified, you get off the ground as quickly and gracefully as you can in the situation. A tall, barefoot guy, in a pair of faded blue jeans, a checked shirt, and glasses hurries toward you.

"Are you okay?" he asks. "I think you're bleeding!"

You lean over and see a big angry bruise forming on your left shin and blood rolling down your right one. "Ow, ow, ow," you say again, looking at your bruised palms.

"I shouldn't have left my boxes out here like this. I'm really sorry. Do you need me to take you to the hospital or something?"

"Ow!"

"At least come inside so we can stop the bleeding. Do you think you can walk?" he asks.

You look up at him, blinking a tear from your eye.

"Wait, let me guess, the answer is 'Ow!'" he says.

❧ If you go into his apartment, go to page 221.

❧ If you just want to hobble home, go to page 233.

◈ Your comfy pants and the movie are calling

Ah, BLISS. HOME AT last. The first thing you do is slip off your heels and dump them on the floor by the front door. Then you pull your dress off over your head, dropping it and your purse on the dressing table as you walk into your bedroom.

You toss your bra and the purple G-string into the laundry hamper in the corner of the room. You'll definitely wear those again, you think. In fact, from now on they may have to be reclassified as your lucky underwear.

Your throw falls short and the little pile of purple lace lands delicately next to the hamper. What the hell, you'll pick it up tomorrow.

You take a long, hot shower, then pull on a pair of regular pants and an oversize T-shirt. You're still too wired from your night out to sleep, and you need to relax. So you stick a bag of popcorn into the microwave—the buttered kind, you've earned it. Then you collapse on the couch and turn on the movie. As the opening credits of *Bridget Jones's Diary* begin to roll, you smile. Life is good. In fact, it doesn't get better than this.

The End

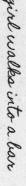

❧ You're not quite ready to go home yet

 IT'S LATE, BUT YOU'RE far too wired to go straight home. You can still feel the last traces of adrenaline pumping through your veins. What a wild night. And to think you were actually considering heading home when Melissa canceled on you earlier this evening. You can hardly believe that was only a few hours ago.

You've been acting completely out of character all night, but you've loved every second of it. You wonder if it was the purple lacy G-string, or being out on your own with nowhere specific to go and nobody but yourself to answer to that made you so daring. Whatever it was, it's been the night of your life.

But now what to do? You wonder if Melissa is still awake—you're dying to tell her what you've been up to. Should you pop over to her place? You're not sure . . . She's probably been asleep for hours. Or you could always stop in at the late-night coffee shop in your neighbor-hood on your way home.

🙠 If you go to the coffee shop on your way home, go to page 242.

🙠 If you decide to go to Melissa's place on your way home, go to page 249.

a girl walks into a bar

❧ You've decided to swing past the late-night coffee shop on your way home

🍸 THE TAXI DROPS YOU off outside the coffee shop. It's so late, it's almost early. The lights are on but other than a bored-looking barista thumbing a smartphone behind the counter, it's empty. You push the door, but it doesn't open. That's odd, you think, they're supposed to be open till really, really late, and it's only just past really late. You push again, but still nothing. You mumble-swear under your breath and then try to catch the barista's eye, but he's doing that pretending-to-be-busy-so-I-don't-have-to-deal-with-you act. Maybe the coffee shop is closed. But then why is he still sitting there? You push against the door again, this time putting your full weight behind it, but it still doesn't budge.

Someone clears their throat behind you, and you

jump. When you turn, there's a guy standing there, about your age, tall, with dark hair and black-rimmed glasses. He's not classically good-looking, but there's something about him. You notice that his mouth skews slightly when he smiles.

"Let me get that for you," he says, reaching for the door handle and pulling it toward you.

"Aha! It's a pull door, not a push door. Um, it's been a long night," you mutter, flushing with mortification.

"Nope, it's not you. I think they might have changed it. I was here two days ago, and it was definitely a push door then. After you," he says, holding the door open for you, as the sounds of Erykah Badu waft from the coffee-shop sound system.

At the counter, he indicates for you to order ahead of him.

"One hot chocolate, please," you say to the barista, who makes a production of putting down his phone and attending to you.

"With marshmallows?" he asks, bored.

Suddenly, ordering a hot chocolate with marsh-mallows seems a little childish, and you're sure you can see the tall guy smirking out of the corner of your eye. First the door, and now this—he must think you have the IQ of a five-year-old. But you decide that, after the night you've had, if you want hot chocolate with marsh-mallows, then that's what you're going to have.

"Yes, please," you say, as confidently as possible. You pay and settle in a chair, riffling through a pile of

a girl walks into a bar

magazines on an adjacent coffee table. You select one at random and pretend to read it while secretly studying the guy over the top of the magazine, eavesdropping as he orders a cappuccino.

He's got a nice body, tall and lean. He's wearing a pair of well-worn jeans, a checked shirt, and a pair of sneakers that he's clearly had for a while. He could do with a haircut and a shave. He turns and catches you checking him out. You dart your eyes back behind your magazine, mortified for the second time.

"Any good?" he asks, and you look up with a show of surprise, as if you've been completely absorbed. He's smiling at you broadly now.

"It's not bad," you say, putting on your best aloof expression.

"So you're in the farming business, then?" he asks.

"What?"

He nods at the magazine, and you see you're holding a copy of *Agriculture Weekly*. And to add insult to injury, it's upside down. You hastily drop it back on the coffee table. "You can never know too much about sheep," you say, trying to recover.

"I guess so," he chuckles. "I count them often."

"Exactly," you say. "And the whole wool thing is pretty impressive. And don't even get me started on fleece!"

"One large cappuccino! One hot chocolate with marshmallows!" shouts the barista, as if the shop were jam-packed. A to-go cup with the word "Cappuccino" written on the side stands on the counter alongside another cup with the words "Hot chocolate" scrawled on it.

You collect your drink, return to your seat, and watch Cappuccino Man surreptitiously as he blows into the hole in the lid of his cup and takes a sip. He looks at it in confusion, then lifts the lid and stares inside. His glasses steam up and he has to put the cup down and take them off to wipe the lenses with the tail of his shirt. He has the longest eyelashes you've ever seen.

He ambles over and places the cup in front of you on the coffee table.

"I think I got yours by mistake," he says.

The cup is clearly marked "Cappuccino," and you give him an inquiring look.

"I almost wasn't going to say anything, it's so damn good," he says, pointing at the marshmallows melting slowly on the top of the hot chocolate inside. "But I thought you'd figure it out sooner or later."

"So by my impressive powers of deduction, this must be yours?" you say, handing him your as-yet-untouched cup.

"Thanks. Of course, you can understand how he got our orders muddled, what with this place being so busy tonight!" he says, waving an arm around the empty shop. The barista has gone back to ignoring you as he reads something riveting on his phone.

You take a sip of your hot chocolate, and he looks into his cup, a little crestfallen.

"Now I have menu envy."

"I'd never sleep if I drank coffee at this hour."

a girl walks into a bar

"That's exactly the effect I was hoping for. I'm busy unpacking; I thought it might help me stay awake for a couple more boxes."

The music comes to an abrupt stop mid-song, and fluorescent lights come on. You shield your eyes and blink as they adjust to the harsh light; nobody looks good in the early hours of the morning under bright lights.

"I guess that means they're closing," he says.

"They're known for their coffee, not for their subtlety," you say.

He pushes the door, holding it open for you with one hand, clutching his hot chocolate–cappuccino in the other.

Outside you pause and look at each other. You get the distinct impression that neither of you is ready to part company just yet. But you feel a little foolish; you can't just stand there. "Well, I suppose it's getting late, or early, rather. I'm going this way," you say, pointing toward your apartment building, which is on the same street, just a few hundred yards away.

"Hey, I'm that way, too. Mind if I walk with you?" he asks.

"You're not an axe murderer or a tax lawyer, are you?"

"Nope, just a writer. I wanted to study axe-murdering at the university, but the class was full."

You laugh, and as you walk, you notice the sky starting to lighten. You can't remember the last time you stayed up all night.

Helena L. Paige

"Well, this is me," you say, stopping at the door to your building.

"Seriously?" he says.

"Yup, but don't worry, I know how this door works, so we should be okay. It's definitely a push."

"This is where I live, too!"

You scrunch your nose up. "Really?"

"Really, I swear, I just moved in a couple of days ago. Number six-ten." And he pulls his keys out of his pocket to show you his key ring. It's one of those generic blue plastic ones, and it has 610 and the name of your building scrawled in the window in blue pen.

"You're kidding! I'm in six-oh-one."

He uses the swipe attached to his key ring to open the security door as proof, then holds the door open for you with a grin on his face. "If I didn't know any better, I'd think you were stalking me," he says.

As you ride the elevator up to your floor, he says, "Since we're neighbors, I thought maybe we could get a drink sometime, and you could show me around the neighborhood? I tasted your hot chocolate—you clearly know what you're doing."

"We could do that."

You both step out of the elevator, and pause. There's a moment of delicious tension.

"Well, I'm this way," you say, nodding toward your door.

"And I'm this way," he says, pointing in the opposite direction. You notice piles of boxes scattered on the carpet outside his apartment. "They're mostly books," he says. "They arrived earlier this evening."

"Well, welcome to the area," you say. "I hope you'll like it here."

"I do already," he says, smiling his sexy crooked smile.

"Night," you say, waving as you walk to your door and let yourself into your apartment, your heart beating just a little faster.

❧ Go to page 238.

Helena S. Paige

❧ You've decided to drop in on Melissa to tell her about your adventures

☙ YOU PRESS THE BUZZER next to her apartment number. You can see from the street that Melissa's bedroom and living room lights are still on, so she must be home. But there's no response when you try her cell. It rings and rings and then goes to voice mail. What is she doing? You're dying to tell her about the crazy night you've had.

You dial again, not caring if you're waking her up. Her phone goes to voice mail again, so you hang up and lean on the buzzer one more time. You don't plan on letting up until she answers.

"Hello?" you hear through the intercom eventually, her voice slightly muffled.

"Finally! Let me in—you won't believe what I've been up to tonight."

There's no response, but the security door buzzes open and you push through into the lobby and take the elevator to Melissa's floor. You tap on her door quietly with the back of a knuckle. It opens at last, but only a crack, so you can just see her face.

"Hey," she says, out of breath, her cheeks flushed.

"Did I wake you up?"

She shakes her head.

"You've got to let me in, I've got so much to tell you!"

"I can't," she whispers, and when she takes her hand off the door to tuck her hair behind her ear you notice a black satin ribbon tied to her wrist. She grins. "You're not going to believe what happened to me, either!"

"What? Wait, have you got somebody in there with you?"

She nods and flushes again.

"Oh my god!" you squeal. "I thought you were working late?"

"I was," she whispers. "But then my boss came back to the office after his meeting, and we started chatting after everyone else left, and then he opened a bottle of wine, and we had a couple of glasses, and, you know, one thing led to another . . ."

"Hang on," you say. "Are you talking about your controlling bastard boss?"

"Shhh!" She giggles. "Yes. But he's not so bad. Turns out we have a lot in common. And I've never said this to you before, but I've always thought he was kind of hot. I mean, aren't all bosses supposed to be a bit controlling and forceful? But when you look beyond that, there's something about this guy . . . It turns out he's totally wild," she says, grabbing your hand, the soft silk tied to her wrist falling against your arm.

"You bad girl!" you say, beaming at her excitement.

"I'm really sorry I stood you up—truly! But it's been one of the wildest nights of my life!"

"Don't be sorry," you say. "It's been a pretty wild night for me, too!"

"Look, I'd better go," she says, glancing back inside the apartment.

"Call me in the morning?"

"It *is* the morning!"

"Later," you laugh, squeezing her hand. You lean in to give her a quick kiss on the cheek, and she smells like a mix of cedar and leather. It's slightly familiar, but you can't quite place it.

Melissa closes her door, and you press the elevator button. At least you weren't the only wild girl tonight. As the elevator arrives, you hear what sounds like a slap from inside Melissa's apartment, leather on naked skin, immediately followed by Melissa's voice crying out, and you can tell it's in pleasure, not pain. You grin again— you can't wait to swap stories.

TIME TO HEAD HOME to contemplate your adventures. But maybe you should stop in and see if your local coffee shop is still open . . .

To head straight home, go to page 217.

To go home via your local late-night coffee shop, go to page 242.

To head straight home, go to page 217.

To go home via your local late-night coffee shop, go to page 242.

Helena L. Paige

❦ You've decided to go home to your Rabbit

🍸 At last, you're standing in the lobby of your apartment building. It's late and your feet are killing you. These heels are supersexy, but there's a price to pay.

There's a pile of cardboard boxes on the floor in front of the elevator, but there's no one nearby. You're curious about who's busy lugging boxes around at this time of the morning, so you lift one of the flaps and peek inside. It's full of books. You can't resist—you pull one out and are peering at the back-cover blurb when the elevator dings open and a man steps out. You stare at each other for a second, and then he says, "Hello. I wasn't expecting a book thief at this hour."

Embarrassed, you drop the book and snatch your hand away. "I wasn't taking it," you explain, flushing.

"No?" he says. "It certainly looks like you were."

Then he smiles and you realize he's teasing you.

"Since you're here, would you mind holding the elevator open for me for a second?" he asks, and you oblige while he picks up the top two boxes. You can't help checking him out as he bends down. The muscles in his arms under his checked shirt flex as he lifts the boxes. He's tall, with dark tousled hair that's just half an inch too long, black-framed spectacles, and a fuzz of early-morning shadow. He's not classically good-looking, but there's something appealing about his slightly crooked smile.

"Who moves this late—or early, more like it?" he comments as he dumps the boxes inside the elevator and goes back for the other two.

"I was wondering about that. Sneaking around moving boxes at this hour, you're either on the run from the police or in witness protection."

"Damn, you've blown my cover," he says as he hefts the last two boxes into the elevator. "Actually, I moved in three days ago. These are the last of my things—they only arrived earlier this evening. But if I'd known how heavy they were, I might have left them behind."

"So you waited till now to move them?"

"I'm a writer, so procrastination is what I do best. I was working late, and I was hoping if I left them down here long enough, they might grow legs and walk upstairs by themselves. Or get stolen. If I hadn't come along when I did, you might have helped with that last option."

You both reach for the sixth-floor button at the same

time and your hands brush. It's like getting a small electric shock, but a good one.

The elevator dings open on the sixth floor, and he motions for you to step out first.

"No, don't worry," you say, leaning against the door. "I'll hold it so you can get your stuff out." You're aware that your motives are not entirely pure: you're offering to help partly so you can admire him hefting boxes for a few more minutes.

"Did you have a fun night?" he asks as he steps past you.

"Not bad," you say, "but I'm glad to be home." The passage is littered with more boxes. "So, we're neighbors, then," you say, stating the obvious.

"Apartment six-ten," he says, putting the box down and pulling a key out of his pocket to show you.

"Apartment six-oh-one," you say, fishing for your own keys in your bag.

"Hey, maybe you could show me around the area sometime?" he says, retrieving the last of his boxes. "I hear there's a fantastic coffee shop down the road."

You're taken aback, but pleasantly so. Is he asking you out? Maybe he is. "Yes, it's pretty good. They make great hot chocolate," you say.

"I'm more of a coffee man myself, but I'm happy to try everything at least once. So hot chocolates are on me. It's the least I can do to thank you for your elevator assistance. How does tomorrow night sound?"

You pretend to think, consulting an imaginary cal-

a girl walks into a bar

endar in your head, while inside you're silently screaming, Yes, I want to lick hot chocolate with extra whipped
cream off your body! You manage a gracious nod:
"Thanks. That sounds like a plan." Then you wave and
walk to your front door. You manage to get the key into
the lock, even though your hands are shaking a little.
Just before you slip inside, you turn and see he's still
standing and watching you, that lopsided smile on his
face.

You're home at last. It's been a strange night. All that
sexual tension and all those false starts have left your
whole body thrumming, in desperate need of relief.

The first thing you do is pull off your shoes and
drop them at the door, then you shed your dress, bra,
and G-string as you walk through your apartment.

You're completely naked by the time you reach your
bedroom, feeling your nipples rise and your breasts
goose-bump as the cool early-morning air slides over
your skin. You run your hand down from your neck,
between your breasts and over your belly, then slide
your fingers between your legs, where you find yourself
hot and wet. You consider lingering, but you want to get
fresh and warm and comfortable first. You need to wash
the night away.

You make the water in the shower as hot as you can
bear it and let it strike the top of your head and run
down your face while you soap your entire body into a
lather.

When you finally step out, after a long, leisurely shower, you wrap yourself in your thickest, thirstiest, most luscious towel.

You brush your teeth, rub your hair dry, and cover yourself from head to toe in body lotion. Then you walk naked through your apartment, turning off all the lights. Finally you slip into bed, luxuriating in the feel of crisp fresh sheets against your bare skin. At the end of the day, there's nothing more blissful than your own bed.

Your heart picks up speed as you slide open the drawer in your bedside table. There's something so naughty about a vibrator. Small ripples of anticipation run through your pussy as you lift out the box and tear open its voluminous packaging.

The Rabbit is the cutest pink color, shaped like a very generous penis, the only difference being the little branch sticking out the side of the shaft, toward the base. You've never seen this design on a vibrator before. The end of the branch contains two little buds that stick out just like bunny ears. You prod them with your finger and they bend under your touch. You reach for the packaging and try to figure out what the little ears are supposed to do. According to the accompanying pamphlet (which gives instructions in French, Japanese, and English), they're clitoral stimulators.

The grip fits snugly in your hand, and just above your thumb are four little buttons with different settings. You press the first button and the gadget vibrates gently against your palm, setting a thrill running through you.

You can't stand the suspense anymore—you've been

a girl walks into a bar

teased and taunted and played with all night, and your body is aching for relief. You can feel the wetness seeping out of you, dampening your thighs as you slip the Rabbit under the covers and run it down your chest on gentle vibrate, tracing the tip of the shaft first over one nipple and then over the other. You squirm as you track the Rabbit farther down your stomach and over your mound.

Then, your breath starting to come a little faster, you place the tip of the vibrator at the very top of your pussy and let the gentle tremors titillate your clit. You let out a small groan, and shift it slightly to the side—it's too intense to have it touching your clit all the time, and you don't want to come just yet.

As slowly as your needy body will allow, you run the vibrator up and down the length of your slit, until it's slipping and sliding in your wetness. Then finally you bend your knees and arch your back as you find your opening and slip it slickly and easily inside you. You use your hand to push it in as far as you want, then pull it back a little. You repeat the action, and as you pump the vibrator deeper, there's an entirely new sensation as the bunny ears massage your clit every time you move your hand.

Suddenly your new neighbor flashes into your head, and you imagine that it's him inside you, his muscular arms braced beside you, holding his weight as he rides you slowly at first, then harder and faster, and you picture that lopsided smile, and feel his fingers on your clit as you push your head back against the pillow.

Helena S. Paige

Ready for more intensity, you shift to the second button with your thumb, and the power goes up a notch, vibrating slightly harder, but it's not enough, so you skip level three and push the Rabbit to its most powerful setting.

You tilt your pelvis upward to meet it every time you plunge it inside you, feeling it vibrating within you, radiating out until you're groaning audibly and bucking your hips, your eyes tight shut, panting, until you can feel your orgasm coming toward you like a runaway train, and you know there's no stopping it. Your toes curl as it shakes through your body, first one orgasm, and then, as you keep the Rabbit going, another. They're so intense that you put both your feet flat down on the bed and brace yourself as the waves of energy course through you.

And then, completely, entirely spent, your damp hair cooling your hot neck on the pillow, you slowly work your way through all the buttons, going from level four back to level one with your thumb, eventually turning it off and dropping your new best friend. You stretch your body out, enjoying the aftershocks. Then you turn onto your side, ready to drift off, with a sigh of satisfaction. Life is good. In fact, it doesn't get better than this.

The End

a girl walks into a bar

ABOUT THE AUTHORS

HELENA S. PAIGE is the pseudonym of authors Helen Moffett, Sarah Lotz, and Paige Nick. **HELEN MOFFETT** wears many hats: freelance writer, editor, researcher, poet, academic, and flamenco fan. **SARAH LOTZ** is a screenwriter and novelist with a fondness for fake names. She writes urban horror novels with author Louis Greenberg under the name S. L. Grey and a YA pulp fiction zombie series with her daughter, Savannah, under the pseudonym Lily Herne. **PAIGE NICK** is an author, award-winning advertising copywriter, and a weekly columnist for the *Sunday Times* (Johannesburg), covering everything from sex to dating and general lunacy.

You're invited . . .

a girl walks into a wedding

by Helena S. Paige

Coming June 2014

Your best friend is getting married and she's asked you to be her bridesmaid. So many decisions. For starters, do you ask the gorgeous but mysterious man you met online to come as your date? Or do you go solo, giving yourself ample opportunity to kick up your heels and scope out the talent?

Once the wedding weekend gets under way in a romantic country setting, all kinds of adventures are on offer. Will you ditch your date? Duet with the hot DJ? Dodge the disreputable best man? Or perhaps the rugged pilot you meet in the bar will open up unexpected erotic opportunities—and who knew the maid of (dis)honor had such a sultry streak?

All this while steering your way through the bachelorette party, the bride's wedding jitters, the Dress from Hell, and more. Perhaps the most tempting option is to flee the entire affair with a tall, dark stranger . . . or maybe an old friend surprises you with a sizzling encounter.

YOU make the decisions—fulfillment guaranteed. It's your fantasy, your rules. The choice is yours . . .